Coyote's Wail

A Peter Joe Mystery
Book 2

by
E. W. Finke

Acknowledgements

I thank my beta readers Elaine Finke and Carolyn Mears for their insightful thoughts and comments on my first draft. I especially thank Karen Brown for her review of my style, pacing, and plot; my editor Virginia Herrick for helping me polish my sentences and stick to editorial standards; and my wife Nadine for her constant encouragement and belief in me.

I also thank Marion Robertson, author of *Red Earth: Tales of the Micmacs*, Nimbus Publishing Limited, Halifax, NS, 1969, for her telling of "The Call of the Loon"; Ruth Holmes Whitehead, author of *Six Micmac Stories,* for her telling of "Woodchuck and the Two Old Women" and "The Boy Who Visited Muini'skw," Nimbus Publishing, Halifax, NS, 1989; First People for its telling of "How Rabbit Got His Long Ears" (https://www.firstpeople.us/FP-Html-Legends/How_Rabbit_Got_His_Long_Ears-Micmac.html, (website no longer available); DRC Publishing, St. John's, NL for permission to use material from Darrin McGrath's *The Newfoundland Coyote,* 2004; the many Mi'kmaw bloggers and authors for their telling of Mi'kmaw history, language, culture, beliefs, and stories; the government of Newfoundland and Labrador; Heritage Newfoundland and Labrador; the scientific, medical, and wildlife communities for information about compound 1080; and those sources listed at the end of the glossary.

Author's Note

A great deal has been written about the history, language, culture, beliefs, and stories of the Mi'kmaq, much of it by the Mi'kmaq themselves. Those writings inform my own storytelling. But I am neither Mi'kmaw nor of any other indigenous or aboriginal descent. I do not speak for the Mi'kmaq or for any other indigenous or aboriginal nation. I make every attempt to use and interpret Mi'kmaw history, language, culture, beliefs, and stories as accurately and respectfully as I can. I apologize to the Mi'kmaq if I err in doing so.

A glossary of Mi'kmaw, Newfoundland, and other words and phrases used in this novel appears near the end.

E. W. Finke

1

Early September, 2005

Eight-year-old Mickey John ran exuberantly ahead of his grandfather, stopped abruptly, and pointed to something at his feet. "What's this, my niskamij?" he called back.

Newfoundland's Bay du Nord Wilderness Reserve was hummocky and rugged, and Mi'kmaw Elder Leon John tottered behind as fast as his eighty-year-old joints would allow. He dropped stiffly to hands and knees to see what Mickey had found. He leaned over it and squinted.

A small red cylinder protruded barely above the ground. A familiar scent triggered a vague image in his mind. *But what is it?* He cursed his flagging memory. He started to warn Mickey away, but before the words came out Mickey kicked it.

The device blew its charge directly into Leon's face. It startled him and he gasped and fell over onto his back. A sudden pain racked his spine. He lay still for a few moments, then wiped his eyes and mouth with his hands. His senses revealed only a light sweetness and a mild irritation in his throat.

Leon saw the fear in Mickey's eyes as Mickey knelt beside him. Leon squeezed his hand. "Go," he uttered faintly, then watched his grandson bolt back down the trail toward the place they had left his father ninety minutes earlier.

Now lying helpless and alone, Leon considered how easy his task had seemed at its beginning. He and Mickey had left Mickey's father, Mark, at the edge of the wilderness for what was to have been a simple hunting lesson. Mark had objected at first, concerned that Leon wasn't strong enough. But Leon would not hear of it. He had insisted it was his duty as both Elder and as Mickey's grandfather to take Mickey into the wilderness alone for this. Reluctantly, Mark had relented.

It had begun at the edge of this very clearing—a twitch of movement that had given away the animal's location. Leon and Mickey had waited patiently for it to reveal itself fully, for to know and respect the animal that would give its life in the hunt was a Mi'kmaw imperative. Reverence for the animal's spirit demanded it be so, and this was the lesson Leon had wanted Mickey to learn today.

The wind had shifted, carrying their scent toward the animal. It had raised its head above the brush and turned to face them directly; a caribou cow with a late-born calf standing quietly nearby.

The first wave of nausea came. Leon forced himself to focus.

It was vital that a Mi'kmaw hunter not separate a mother from its young, and he had beamed at the prospect of conveying this second lesson in the same encounter. To that end, he had pushed himself to his full height and had watched as the cow and its calf had bounded off. Loudly enough for Mickey to hear, Leon had wished them both a long and healthy life.

Then had come the moment Leon had hoped for. Mickey had stood, waved, and called out quietly, "Long life, my relations." That was when Mickey had run ahead.

Leon decided that he had succeeded; he had given Mickey what he needed to thrive as an apprentice hunter. "Our people will honor him," he said softly. The nausea grew more intense now, but he smiled with pride.

The muscles of his frame began to tighten and spasm. He retched and convulsed and thrashed as a fall rain began to patter the leaves around him. He steeled himself against the pain, but he sensed he had not long to live. He closed his eyes and prepared himself for a life forevermore in the Next World.

2

One week later

I had just boarded the Newfoundland and Labrador Fish and Wildlife Department's helicopter, snapped my harness, and adjusted my headset when wildlife officer Mitchell Gregg turned toward me from the pilot's seat and fumed

"Damn shame if you ask me, Chief! Once certain people get it in their heads to blame somethin' for their troubles, they don't care to know the real problem. Same in the 60s when the cod were fished to extinction. 'It's the harp seals takin' 'em!' they said. 'Anybody can't see that's a damn fool! Better to kill 'em off now than be wastin' all that tax money studyin' things, eh, b'y?'" He sighed. "Some people're just a little too ignorant for my liking."

From the bits of Mitchell's radio call I had overheard, it seemed that one of his superiors had given him an earful of Assemblyman Carson "Hunter" Sullivan's complaints about how Mitchell's department was bungling yet another problem. Sullivan represented the Fortune Bay-Cape La Hune riding, which meant he also represented my Mi'kmaw First Nation. I'd not met him, but he had the reputation of a man full of his own importance.

"Oh, and that's Lucie Headley behind you," he said more calmly. "Wildlife biology intern, damn good one. First trip out. Lucie, Mi'kmaw Chief Peter Joe."

"Nice to meet you, Chief Joe," she said.

I turned to her and smiled. "My pleasure, Lucie. Good to have you along." She looked to be about nineteen and just over five feet tall. She'd pulled her straight black hair behind her head into a ponytail and had fed it over the strap at the back of her cap. She wore oval glasses with black frames on a pale face, and a new-looking field uniform.

I turned back around and stared out my side window. I knew Mitchell well and we had worked together many times before, but I was disquieted about this particular job. According to the message he'd left me just last evening, we'd be checking out a telephone tip he'd received about an illegal kill on ancestral Mi'kmaw land.

Mitchell throttled up for takeoff. The turbine whined and the rotors wound up to the rapid-fire *chop* of flight. My seat push me upward and, in what seemed like only a moment, we were well over the trees and headed northeastward.

Eight years my senior, at forty-three Mitchell was lean and fit, a likeable man with an easy manner. But I also knew him to be one who didn't hide his disdain for the contradictions and hypocrisies in others. He invariably wore his blue-gray department uniform even on his days off. Today, he had exchanged his usual black shoes for more rugged boots and left the tie behind.

It was a clear, cool fall morning. The sun began to warm us as Mitchell turned eastward. Below us, small water pockets, ponds, lakes, and streams, separated here and there by stands of scrawny spruce, littered the rocky barrens.

A short while later, we descended over an open field and landed. I stepped out of the cockpit onto a small part of the Bay du Nord Wilderness Reserve.

I knew this place well and I ordinarily would have eagerly welcomed an invitation to stand here again. As a boy, I'd spent countless summer hours in this wilderness with my father. The memories of our times here returned as though I had been here just yesterday—silent valleys densely laden with balsam fir, tranquil river threads and crashing waterfalls, the deafening honk and wingbeat of hundreds of Canada geese taking flight all at once, and the thunder of woodland caribou herds as big as the land itself.

For my father, Abram Jeddore, then Chief of the Mi'kmaq First Nation, this was a place of great solace, a temporary escape from the seemingly endless battle for respect from the provincial government. Today, after having taken his place as Chief one year ago, I felt the warmth and the welcome of this place calm me deeply, just as it must have done for him then, and just as I imagined it had done for the Old Ones for centuries before.

But as I turned around to see why Mitchell had brought me here, an all-consuming anger suddenly boiled up within me. I felt hot and my gut tightened. It took all I had to keep my emotions hidden.

Before me lay three bald eagles, dead and scattered in a wide circle at the edge of the clearing. One lay on its side, curled into a disheveled fetal ball. Another lay splayed out and face down, wings broken and twisted as if it had beaten them wildly on the rocks and brush. The third hung from a bush from a blood-stained wing, its body and other wing dangling limply below. A fourth eagle, still alive, thrashed itself along the ground as if in grand mal convulsions.

How is this possible? And why? All life has meaning, and this was a great insult on that account alone. But the eagle has always held a special, sacred place for us—Kitpu is the envoy of our deepest prayers to Kji-Niskam.

At the center of this wretched scene lay the carcass of a caribou buzzing with the drone of stouts and black flies. It had the stench of a death already days old.

On the other side of the carcass, Lucie had already donned on a pair of latex gloves and a surgical mask. She carefully collected samples of tissue and a white residue from the areas where the eagles appeared to have been feeding and placed them into small glass jars. She labeled each jar and made notes as she went. Periodically, she turned away and sucked in a breath of air that her face told me was only slightly better. Then she buried the jars in the ice-filled cooler.

Mitchell squatted beside the carcass, seemingly unaffected by the reek and carnage. I knelt beside him to get a closer look.

The animal's hide had been peeled back at the belly and flanks in a way no animal could have done. Mitchell pulled a white latex glove onto his right hand and scanned the carcass intently. He pushed his index finger into a small hole in its side, just about where I would have expected its heart to be.

"Bullet," he murmured as he withdrew his finger. He stood. "What do you make of it, Lucie?"

"Too hard to say right now, Mr. Gregg. Could be a neurotoxin or some kind of pesticide, maybe. But I'll hold my answer till I get the lab results."

I was impressed by her. She seemed inquisitive and cautious in her conclusions.

Mitchell sighed as we moved to examine one of the eagle carcasses. “Got notice about this late yesterday afternoon,” he said. “My guess? Caribou was killed, laced with poison, set out as bait. Predator poisoning is still illegal in this province.”

“But who would poison eagles?” I asked. I still struggled to stay calm inside.

He pulled the latex glove from his hand by the cuff, sealed it inside a small plastic bag, and pushed the bag into his left-side jacket pocket. “Somebody after coyotes, I suspect. Or wolves. Eagles just got here first this time.”

“Wait, coyotes or wolves?”

He grinned. “Yep, lot happened here while you were off on the mainland, Chief.”

I knew he meant the nineteen years I had tried to adapt to white culture after my Quebecois mother took me from the Mi’kmaq reserve to Montreal when I was fifteen. I’d come to know him well over the past year and recognized his remark as a friendly barb.

“So, fill me in,” I said.

“Well, they first came in ’85. March it was. A now long-retired wildlife officer got a call about three wolves sittin’ on the ice at the south end of Port au Port Peninsula. But wolves’d been extinct here more than eighty years, right? So he and his partner flew out there to see for themselves. Didn’t see any wolves, just tracks in the snow. The gulf was frozen all the way to Cape Breton that year and that’s where those tracks seemed to come from.

“Think about that. A hundred eighty kilometers, give or take. Roughly fifteen days on the ice with no guaranteed source of food or water. Hugely resourceful animals we’re talking about here!

"Anyway, a year later a trapper near Bay of Islands caught what turned out to be a coyote pup, an' a Deer Lake trapper caught three adult males."

"So those wolves on the ice, they were really coyotes?" Lucie interjected.

"Sure were," Mitchell answered, "but they're a hell of a lot bigger than you'd think, upwards of thirty-five kilos for some. And now true wolves are comin' back, too, prob'ly across the ice from Labrador. And they're interbreedin' with our bigger-than-usual coyote friends, makin' 'em even bigger. Coy-wolves we call 'em."

He ended there and gestured toward the helicopter. "Give me a hand?"

Lucie and I stood and followed him, but his words were almost too strange to believe. Coyote held a prominent place in many native cultures, but it had not lived among my people. The Old Ones had given Mi'kmawisimk no word for this animal.

We returned with four small body bags. The fourth eagle had died, so Mitchell and Lucie bagged each of them and stowed the bags in the helicopter's refrigerated bin. Under our agreement with the provincial government, eagles found dead on traditional Mi'kmaw lands were to be entrusted to my people. But the department would autopsy these eagles first.

Mitchell asked if I would mind tagging along to his next destination before returning to my reserve. I learned that today was opening day of coyote hunting season, and his department had boosted its regular field officer assignments. Mitchell's detail was already on location, and he wanted to check on them.

Lucy and I snapped our harnesses and donned our headsets. Mitchell busied himself with the details of preparing for flight while the rotors wound up from a dull *foof* to their staccato *chop*. I heard him tell someone on the radio what we had found and give coordinates for a team to retrieve the carcass.

I turned away and stared blankly at the wilderness outside my window. Only a few days ago, my people and I had buried a beloved Elder. Now I faced having to tell them that four Kitpu had died in nearly the same place. It would not be a good afternoon.

3

We flew west, gaining altitude steeply to both clear the trees and to avoid disturbing the geese and caribou. Seeing this land from above gave me an entirely new perspective, but it was still the most spectacular country I could imagine.

We were now almost directly over route 360 at its junction with 365, the spur beside Bay d'Espoir leading to the homes and buildings of Conifer, my village and the center of my reserve. Mitchell eased up on the throttle, pushed himself into the back of his seat, and picked up where he'd left off earlier.

"So, ranchers say those animals are killing their sheep just for the practice. Outfitters say they're takin' out all the caribou and moose calves, an' they'll be driven out of business. If we listened to them, we'd be killin' off every coyote and wolf around. But lotsa things affect the herds, right? Disease, mining, logging, power lines, fire, food abundance. And bears . . . we know they prey on them, too."

He paused to make a small adjustment to our heading. "Studies say we'd have to cut the population by seventy percent or more to have any lasting effect, an' keep it that low year after year. There's no way good way to do that without a province-wide intervention that'd end up killin' other wildlife, too."

"Mr. Gregg," Lucie interrupted, "if wolves and coyotes aren't really the problem, why is there such a big misunderstanding?"

"Good question. One, people look for what agrees with what they already believe and ignore what doesn't. Second, coyotes an' wolves are still pretty new here. The trouble is the war stories about 'em that come from away. An' then, license and tax revenues from outfitters and hunters are a bright light in this economy, and they know how to throw their weight around. My point bein' that we don't have to wait until they're such a problem that there's no choice but killin' 'em off by the thousands. We're in a place right now to handle 'em with honest assessments and thoughtful management strategies."

"That suggests we'll probably see more of what we saw today," I said.

Mitchell gave me a knowing glance. "That'd be my guess, too."

He eased off the throttle and put us into a descending spiral toward the west end of a large clearing beside Ahwachanjeesh Pond. A breeze jostled the cabin but Mitchel expertly kept us oriented for landing. A group of people on the other side of the clearing momentarily looked up at us as we descended.

I waited until the rotors died, then climbed down out of the cockpit. Lucie said she would stay to complete chain-of-custody paperwork for the eagles and tissue samples she'd collected. Raised voices reached us as Mitchell and I walked toward the crowd at the east end of the gravelly clearing. I began to get a better picture of what I had seen from above.

What I'd taken for one group was actually two, facing off. One group wore camouflage; I assumed they were the coyote and wolf hunters Mitchell would have expected to see here today. I counted twelve.

The fifteen demonstrators wore yellow SAVE THE PREDATORS! Vests, or green REMEMBER EARTH DAY shirts, and carried signs declaring KEEP IT WILD NEWFOUNDLAND, END THE SLAUGHTER, and MAN IS THE REAL PREDATOR!

The demonstrators wielded branches, and the hunters carried hunting rifles strapped behind a shoulder or long-barreled pistols holstered to a hip. Bodies stiffened and jaws jutted as they simultaneously bellowed out slogans and shouts laced with profanities. A few of the hunters brandished their rifles in the air.

Standing alone about ten meters away, a woman seemed to be content with just observing the action. A camera hung around her neck, as if she had come for a day of scenic photography but had been interrupted by the clamor in front of her.

In the center of the clearing, ten pickup trucks with mud-splashed off-road tires stood in a semicircle directly behind the hunters. They seemed to have been arranged to confront the demonstrators as menacingly as the hunters themselves.

Between these two factions stood a line of three wildlife officers attempting to deescalate the confrontation. One officer faced the hunters, the second the demonstrators, the third the hunters again. They looked nervous.

Mitchell announced his intention to help his officers calm the crowd, but before he could take his first step a black sedan hurtled toward us. We stepped back as it skidded to a halt where we'd just been standing, spewing gravel and raising a cloud of dust that followed the breeze into our faces. My breath stopped and my eyes squeezed shut.

When the dust passed, the passenger side front door swung sharply open. A short, balding man with pale skin and a soft, thick build emerged and adjusted a red bow tie in the side mirror. He donned a pair of sunglasses, slammed the door, and swaggered straight to Mitchell. Mitchell gave me a subtle roll of his eyes.

"Why, if it ain't Mitchell Gregg," said Swagger Man. "One of our government's finest, I should say!" He planted his hands on his hips and scanned the scene.

"I see you and your b'ys is doin' a fine job here, Mitchell," he continued. "Ain't every day I watch a pack of undesirables harass our dear province's law-abiding outdoorsmen exercising deir god-given rights to a legal hunt. I'm certain you're here to end dis abomination and send dese petty folks on deir way, am I right? Dey've no business here, Mitchell. No business at all."

"Assemblyman Sullivan. How nice to see you again," Mitchell replied with sarcasm. "I see no cause to eject these people from the crown's land. They got the same right to be here as you and I. An' I believe you know that."

"Nonsense, Mitchell! Flailin' branches at dem poor b'ys, causing a ruckus. No doubt dey've driven off every coyote around here, spoiled an otherwise fine first day for dese men.

"And de worst of it is most of them come from away! More than likely, those b'ys spent two week's pay getting ready for dis day, what with license fees and all. You need me to remind you where dose fees go? Directly to your department is where. Which by my reckoning means you owe dese b'ys some protection from dis harassment."

"Branches are no match for firearms," Mitchell responded. "And the law still says license fees are for research, habitat management, and code enforcement, not police protection for your supporters. You know that, too."

Sullivan seemed at a sudden loss for words because he glared blankly at Mitchell. Then he turned to face me, as if my presence had caught him by surprise. "And who's dis man?"

"Chief Peter Joe, Saqamaw of the Mi'kmaq First Nation," I answered.

"Hmph." He scowled at me for what seemed like minutes. "I knew your father. Made a lot of trouble, seems to me."

I met his eyes with a straight face, but I steamed inside. "You knew nothing about my father, seems to me."

His face began to turn red. He looked like he was about to say more, but he was distracted by Standalone Woman who had moved closer and had begun to photograph the entire scene—the demonstrators, the hunters, the exchanges between us and Assemblyman Sullivan, even the helicopter. It seemed she wasn't here for the scenery after all.

Sullivan broke his glare at me to pose next to Mitchell with a smile. She took their photograph from a short distance away. Then he stepped back, regained his scowl, and continued his tirade.

"So you say, Mitchell. Let us see what your superiors say about dis when I report your behavior. Dere's too long been a wrong-headed focus in your division. Coyotes, wolves—nothin' but varmints. Infected with mites, ticks, intestinal parasites . . . an' more god-awful things than anyone can name. Good for nothing but killing sheep and caribou, and dey'll be de end of dis economy if dey don't kill us first! For twenty years hunters and ranchers been waiting for your department to do something, and nothing got done but studying 'em until God knows when.

"But a new law's gonna make a change for de better, eh? You'll get a new mission soon! And sooner you rid de province of dem freeloaders, de better off we'll all be. Just like dem people over dere." He swung his right arm at the demonstrators. "Come from away and got no business here!"

Sullivan huffed out a large breath of air. "In de meantime," he continued, pointing his finger at the crowd, "what's needed over dere is someone to take matters into hand. And seeing as no one else is doing it"—he raised himself onto his toes and attempted to look Mitchell in the face—"I guess it's up to me." With that, Sullivan dropped back onto his heels and swaggered off toward the crowd. Standalone Woman took a few more photographs as he began to interact with them.

"What was that about?" I asked Mitchell.

He muttered something under his breath. "Cocky little bastard" is what it sounded like, but I didn't ask him to repeat it.

"Sullivan tabled a so-called predator-hunting bill in the Assembly, with a bounty that'd make it profitable to just kill them off. Made it through second reading in spring sitting, but got preempted by an emergency funding bill. But he'll table it again fall sitting for sure. 'This is the greatest ecological crisis in the history of Mother Canada,' he told them, 'and it's our moral duty to respond with decisive certainty!' Like he was preachin' to a congregation.

"It'll hit the good people in my division hardest. All that experience and progress over decades, gone. 'License, please,' is the only management we'll be doin'." He sighed and shook his head.

I couldn't believe what I had just heard. Mitchell had become an ally on natural resource matters where our ancestral lands, our people, and our customs were involved. He'd gone out of his way to be sure I or someone from our First Nation was involved at every step. He'd shown a committed respect for Mi'kma'ki and the generations of ecological knowledge my people had gained here. And he'd earned my trust. I was about to ask him if all of that was suddenly for nothing when Standalone Woman lowered her camera and walked toward us.

"Hey, Mitchell," she said. "That was quite a tongue lashing!"

She was shorter than both Mitchell and me, but she still would have dwarfed Sullivan. She had large brown eyes and a rounded nose set in a tanned face. A ball cap with a MONTREAL CANADIENS insignia on the front rode on top of dark brown hair that hung loosely on the back of her neck. I guessed her to be in her mid-twenties.

"H'lo, Emma. Good to see at least one person came with a decent disposition. But how'd you know?"

"It's good to see you here today, too. My editor told me to be here, he even knew the time. You didn't get the word?"

"Hmph. Not exactly. But I should've guessed somethin' mighta been up today … Oh, sorry. Chief, Emma Walsh, brand new special investigations reporter for the News-Advertiser at Grand Falls-Windsor. Emma, Chief Joe, Mi'kmaq First Nation at Conifer."

We shook hands. "My pleasure," she said.

"Likewise," I responded.

She turned back to Mitchell. "Mitchell, ever since Sullivan first tabled his new predator-hunting bill, I've gotten a lot of calls, and I've often called you about them. It seems like some people feel more comfortable reporting what they see or hear to a journalist rather than the authorities. I had a call like that just this morning before I left my office, a darn strange one. I hope you can help me understand it."

"Do my best, Emma. What is it?"

"It was a woman," she began. "And her son. She sounded pretty old to me, but seemed to be pretty independent—she lives beside a lake on Little River in a cabin with only her Catahoula dog. Her son also lives beside it but a little south of her. She has no telephone, so her son drove her to Milltown-Head of Bay d'Espoir to make her call. She said she likes our news service, so it was us she thought of. The receptionist gave her call to me.

"She said her dog has a habit of running off when it gets the notion, and it often returns with what she called 'a treasure from the woods." Yesterday afternoon, it came back with a man's forearm in its mouth. She was quite shocked, of course, and she asked her son to track the dog's trail back to where it found the arm. He was able to do that, and there he found a young man dressed in camouflage lying dead beside a lake about five kilometers from her house. He assumed a fox or lynx had been working on the dead man's arm and had been scared off when such a large dog arrived.

"Her son could not forget the look in the man's eyes, 'still open and etched with the last screams of his life,' she said. He'd told her the man's arms and legs were splayed out stiffly and the grass and brush around him were torn up, as if the man had thrashed around before he died.

"And then came the most puzzling part. She said he'd found a small metal stake in the ground and an empty bullet cartridge lying nearby. Just one, and a small piece of red cloth. Yet the son found no sign of a gun, blood, or even a wound. He left those things where he found them, assuming they would be evidence for the authorities.

"I've already told the RCMP about this, but it's good that I've found you here." She paused, as if waiting for the information she had just conveyed to sink in.

"So, what do you think?" she ended.

"Well . . . no idea. That's it, eh? Nothin' else?"

I suddenly felt a chill run down the back of my neck. "You're sure about that, Emma? That's almost the same as the story I was given last week. A boy from my reserve had been out with his grandfather in the Bay du Nord a week ago. Something made him run back for his father in a panic. When the boy and his father returned to the grandfather, they found him dead. The boy was traumatized and hasn't spoken a word to anyone one ever since.

I turned to Mitchell. "Search and Rescue described the grass and brush torn up around him and his body contorted, just like Emma described. I didn't say anything to you earlier because RCMP found no sign of foul play, and the coroner ruled it a natural death. But it happened somewhere beside Medonnegonix, not far from where we were earlier today, and not far from Little River. Neither RCMP nor Search and Rescue said anything to us about finding a cartridge, but—" I stopped abruptly, thinking about what all this might mean. "I need to check this out, Mitchell. I'd like to get back."

Emma's brows rose slightly and she spoke before Mitchell could answer. "And I'd like to meet you there, Chief Joe. This is something our readers need to know about."

"Come in two days, Emma. I need time with my chief of police first."

Emma nodded and I looked again at Mitchell, anticipating an answer. He seemed to hesitate.

"I need some time with my guys first," he said, glancing at the crowd. "Looks like they could use a hand breakin' things up over there." He walked off to join his officers. Sullivan was still there, and he seemed to be in a confrontation with one of the demonstrators. Mitchell spoke to his three officers, then all four began to move the two factions apart. Gradually, the hunters and demonstrators dispersed and moved to their vehicles. Sullivan yelled something to each group as they did.

"Okay, let's get airborne," Mitchell said when he returned.

As the engine wound up, I stared out my window and once again tried to make sense of things. A grandfather and respected Elder dead, ruled a natural death. Four sacred messengers to Kji Niskam poisoned by a carcass intended for coyotes or wolves. Now, Armless Man. Another natural death? Another accident? An Old Ones' teaching story came to mind.

Suddenly, Munmkwej the woodchuck leapt from the boiling pot, grabbed his hide from the tanning frame, and ran from the wigwam into the woods laughing.

Things were not as they seemed, I knew that now. My seat rocked as we lifted off, and I watched the ground fade away below me.

* * * * *

Carson "Hunter" Sullivan, Minister of the Newfoundland and Labrador House of Assembly for the Fortune Bay-Cape La Hune riding, strode confidently toward the demonstrators. The din of voices grew louder as he approached. He elbowed his way into the middle of the crowd and directed himself to the three wildlife officers.

"OK, b'ys, MHA Hunter Sullivan. I'll take it from here. You b'ys go on about your business somewhere else," he told them.

One of them looked toward Mitchell Gregg, but Mitchell was engaged with two other people and didn't notice. They ignored Sullivan.

"Go on, now! You ain't needed here no more!" Sullivan yelled, but the officers stood their ground, keeping the groups separated.

Sullivan turned to face the demonstrators. "All right, fun's over! Take your petty signs and slogans back where you came from! A bunch of fousties, all of you! He shooed them away like mongrel dogs. "Now git!"

"Yeah! Go on back where ya belong!" shouted one of the hunters. He stepped forward to stand beside Sullivan and glared at the demonstrators. "Or face the business end of my friend!" he added, brandishing his rifle over his head. Sullivan smiled and thanked him with a pat on the back. The man gave Sullivan a nod and an outsized grin.

Sullivan's boldness took the demonstrators by surprise, and they quieted. The hunters followed suit. A demonstrator with long, dark hair and wearing denim jeans and shirt under an open gray trench coat stepped forward out of the crowd. The demonstrator began to speak, but Sullivan interrupted.

"Still plannin' on having some of your twisted fun, are ya, young fella?" he challenged.

The demonstrator looked Sullivan directly in the face. "I know who you are, and you have no authority here, you coyote killer."

"An' I know exactly who you are, too," retorted Sullivan. "Matter of fact, I'da been disappointed you didn't show up. But you're a foreign trespasser in the affairs of my province. You know nothing about 'em, and you got no business here. So take your pack of mangy friends and git home." He thumbed at the hunters behind him. "I'll handle dese b'ys myself."

The demonstrator leaned in and glared. "We're not going anywhere until I say so, Sullivan!"

"Da'd be *Minister Hunter* Sullivan if ya please, mister save-de-predators Ross Nelson. And you'll be standing dere for quite a time, because new law's gonna say coyotes and wolves are worthless varmints. And just like 'em, you and your friends ain't wanted here either. Dese b'ys behind me are here for a day of fair and legal sport, and you're interfering. 'Obstructing de conduct of a legal act' would be a lawyer man's words for it. So pack your things and git yourselves home before I call de RCMP to do it for you. An' dey know me well, so if you're thinking 'bout being smart-assy again, don't trouble yourself."

Nelson glared back at Sullivan, but was interrupted when Mitchell Gregg wove his way through the crowd to the other three officers. Mitchell spoke to them briefly, then turned to Nelson and his team.

"You got a right to demonstrate, but I have to ask you all to move away and let these men proceed," he said. "They're within their legal right to hunt here. Your issue with 'em would better be addressed in the Assembly."

Nelson hesitated and Sullivan took advantage. He grinned proudly. "Well, ain't that just what I been sayin', junior." He turned to Mitchell. "And da'd be de first sensible thing I heard from you today. I'm grateful."

Mitchell didn't respond and instead turned to face the hunters. "And you. We don't look kindly on this behavior from the people we issue licenses to. I suggest you be on your way before we pull every one of 'em."

Nelson gave a frustrated sigh. "OK, let's pack it up for today, team." He then addressed Sullivan. "We're leaving, but don't for a minute think this is the last you'll see of us. We're in this for the long fight. We stood against your sad little debacle when it began, and we'll be standing there when it dies!" He made a slit-throat motion with his hand.

Sullivan stared back without expression. "Every man got his own delusions, sonny. Be on your way, now."

The demonstrators dispersed to their cars and drove off, and all four wildlife officers left the scene.

Wide grins appeared on the hunters' faces and they congratulated one another with fist bumps and vigorous slaps on the back.

Sullivan laughed as he watched. "Pansies!" he shouted after the demonstrators.

"An' you fellas," he called out to the hunters, "Dere's coyotes out dere, b'ys! An' dey're just waitin' for you!"

Some of the still-grinning hunters went to their trucks and roared off; others grabbed their gear and disappeared into the woods. A sole unsmiling hunter stayed behind.

When the last of the others had gone, Sullivan and the one remaining hunter stood together watching the helicopter finish its climb.

"You and your b'ys done a fine job here, Damon," Sullivan said at last. He pulled a brown envelope from a pocket inside his suit coat and tried to slip it into Damon's hand.

Damon Duffy brushed the envelope aside without looking at it. Sullivan put it back into his pocket and simply nodded.

4

Dawn had not yet given way to sunrise as I approached our administration building, the long, white, two-story building with the peaked center that stood beside the south bank of the Conifer River. My second-floor office window looked out over the Conifer's wide, lazy mouth; I could not imagine a more serene view. Nor one that spoke more deeply of our history here, for just beyond my window lay the very place my people had first hauled their canoes onto the southern shore of Ktaqamkuk to fish and hunt for the next many hundreds of years.

I entered the building, took care of a minor piece of paperwork on my desk, and walked down the hall to the office of Police Chief Clarence Paul. The aging wooden floors creaked and moaned under my footsteps—a sound that had greeted me from my very first day as Saqamaw. I welcomed it, and I sometimes walked the floor just to hear it. It helped me clear my mind, like talking with an old friend.

It was not yet seven a.m., and Clarence's door was still locked, as I had expected. I settled onto the bare wooden bench beside his door and pulled the brim of my cap down over my face. I closed my eyes and crossed my arms and legs. I drifted into deep thought about the unwelcome news of the last few days: Leon John, the four sacred Kitpu, and

Armless Man. Something inside told me there must be a common factor, some connection between these events.

Leon had been a wise, patient, and caring man, loved and respected by every member of our First Nation. Not a single one had missed his Salite. In the past year, I had come to know Leon well myself, and I had welcomed his wise counsel as I grew into the position of Saqamaw. I had comforted his family as best I could, but I knew well the grief of losing a cherished family member, as it had been only a little more than a year ago that my own father died for reasons I still can't entirely explain.

Leon's family was close-knit and he had always been present for them, always there for the whole. The bond between Leon and his grandson Mickey John had been particularly strong, and it was Mickey who had taken his passing the hardest. Even now, a week after his grandfather's death and despite the patient encouragement of family and friends, Mickey has refused to leave his room and spoken to no one. I made a mental note to check in on him soon. Perhaps the similarity of our losses could help repair his broken spirit.

Uneven footsteps and a tap at the sole of my boot stirred me.

"Still sleepin'?" I heard, then a chuckle.

I lifted the brim of my cap to see Clarence Paul unlocking his office door.

"Should'a had a coffee this mornin', Chief," he said, grinning on his way inside. "Piskwa'."

I stood and took a long stretch. *Maybe he's right*. I entered his office to see him unholster his sidearm, stash it in his top left desk drawer, then lock the drawer. His only office trappings were three old but neat file cabinets behind the desk, a large family photo on the desk's left corner, and a small plaque displaying a gold, four-pointed star on its right.

"Weli eksitpu'k, Chief," he said.

"Weli eksitpu'k, Chief," I replied.

Clarence was a stocky man with dark, short-cropped hair and a receding hairline. I knew him as a frank man who valued integrity as a fundamental necessity of human character, but a man with a quick humor, too. Of his nine years with Canadian Forces, the three overseas had brought him both that Star of Military Valor and an uneven stride, and he was proud of both. He'd said two years of law school told him he didn't want to practice but they prepared him well for the RCMP's Police Academy. Since then, he'd served every day of his policeman's life on our reserve, including his appointment as Chief of Police under my father.

Like Leon, Clarence had been particularly influential during my first year as Saqamaw. He was twenty years my senior, but we related as equals. He'd become a sort of confidante, someone I could bounce policy ideas off, strategize with, and talk about what-ifs knowing that our conversations would be completely confidential.

He sat down into the wooden chair behind his desk and pointed his open hand to an identical chair beside it. "Pa'si. What brings you?" he said.

I sat. "You were there when RCMP combed the location where our Elder died, am I right?"

"I was. Spent the morning out there. Why?"

"Could RCMP have missed anything?"

"Don't think so. They sent O'Neill. He's a pretty thorough guy. I was with him every step, and when he interviewed Search and Rescue, too. Even did some looking around myself."

"Well, I think he missed something."

"That'd be unlikely." He paused with a puzzled look on his face. "What's on your mind, Chief?"

"Well, two things. Yesterday, I learned a man died beside a lake up on Little River. What caught my attention was where and how he was found. Just like our Elder—in the wild, face contorted, arms and legs hyper-extended, and signs he had thrashed around on the ground. Only difference was that a cartridge was found nearby this one. Empty, but apparently no sign the man had died from a bullet wound. Except for that casing, the circumstances of his and our Elder's deaths were almost the same. So I was thinking it would be worth having a second look where he died. Maybe there was a casing there, too, but RCMP overlooked it because his thrashing had buried it somewhere."

"It was RCMP that told you about this Little River fella?" he asked.

"No, a reporter. I met her yesterday while out with Mitchell Gregg." I told him Emma's story about the old woman and Armless Man.

He thought for a few moments. "And the second?"

"The reason I was out with Mitchell Gregg at all yesterday was because he'd received a tip about an illegal kill in the Bay du Nord Wilderness. That's on our traditional lands, so he flew me out there with him." I told him about the carcass and the eagles.

"What caught my attention about this was that the dying eagle thrashed around on the ground while it was dying, just like our Elder and that other dead man seem to have done. And the other eagles looked as if they had done the same."

"Anyway, I think where our Elder died deserves another look. I think there's a connection between him, the eagles, and Armless Man," I finished.

Clarence sat back into his chair, appearing to digest what I had just told him.

"Well, for the first," he began at last, "it seems what you have is the account of an old woman living in the wilderness who you didn't speak to and her son also living in the wilderness who you also didn't speak to, as told by a reporter you met only yesterday."

My eyebrows went up.

"I'd question why they chose to call a reporter and not RCMP. Seems odd to me, like maybe they were bored, cooked up a scheme to get some attention, see what kind of a scare they might get into the media."

He sighed. "Since there's some possibility it's legit, I'll follow up with RCMP. But I already know what they'll say. They're shorthanded. Took 'em two days to check out our Elder's scene. And I got no influence unless we know the dead man was one of ours. Long story short, I'd say they'll get to it when they get to it.

"As to the second, it looked to me like our Elder just collapsed onto the ground."

"I think there's more to it."

Clarence leaned back into his chair and cupped his hands over the ends of its armrests. "Well, I can see you're suspicious. But suspicion isn't enough, right? It takes evidence, and RCMP was pretty thorough. Had he thrashed around before he died? Maybe, but coulda been a couple caribou or a moose bedded that area the night before. Was he rigid and contorted when Search and Rescue found him? Well yeah, but some of us go hard, and he was in rigor mortis. You and I'll probably be contorted and stiff when we die, too."

He leaned forward and looked at me directly. "Chief, I get how you feel about him. He was dear to all of us, and I miss him, too. But we have to face it." He opened his hands. "He was old. We all die when we get old."

I heard sympathy in his voice and his words held me. I began to question my own thinking. *Were the similarities I saw just the workings of my imagination? Had I jumped to a conclusion?* I sat back with folded arms and stared at the floor.

Clarence began again. "As for the eagles, they're not a matter for us—police-wise, I mean. Best to leave that end of things in Mitchell Gregg's hands. But folks here were already devastated by our Elder's passing; it's been a hard time for all. When they hear four Kitpu were killed, too . . . well, might be best we had a sweat. Up to you."

I nodded. "I already made Jason the sweat conductor on this one."

Clarence nodded back. "Good call."

"Last question," I said. "Exactly where did our Elder die?"

He pulled a map from his drawer, unfolded it onto the top of his desk, and put his finger beside Medonnegonix Lake. "Right here. West shore, northern tip. RCMP yellow-taped it in case they had to come back."

We sat in silence silent for nearly half a minute. I stood, stretched again, and pushed my hands into my pockets. "Well, that's it then, isn't it?" I said.

"Seems so."

I nodded again, then started toward the door.

"But you don't believe any of it, do you?" he said. He knew me too well.

"Can't say that I do," I called back with a grin he couldn't see.

5

Ross Nelson stared disconsolately through a street-side window inside the Tim Horton's on Quinpool Road in Halifax and washed down the last of a honey cruller with a long draw of original blend. What troubled him at the moment was what he'd just read in the copy of Grand Falls-Windsor's *News-Advertiser* that he'd bootlegged from the Gander airport on his way back to Halifax.

> **PREDATOR WAR HEATS UP**
> *Emma Walsh, News-Advertiser*
>
> Amid increasing controversy over Newfoundland's growing coyote and wolf populations, hunters and demonstrators faced off yesterday on opening day of the Island's fourth regular coyote hunting season. Pro and con forces clashed at Awachanjeesh Pond, the entrance to a popular trapping and hunting area.
>
> The willingness of demonstrators to confront hunters directly has been spurred by rising concern over a year-round, no-bag-limit, predator-hunting bill sponsored by MHA Carson Sullivan of the Fortune Bay-Cape La Hune riding. Seasons are currently limited to ten months for coyote (unlimited

bag) and five months for wolf (bag limit one). If approved, the bill would remove bag limits and authorize provincial bounties of $300 for wolves and $175 for coyotes, replacing the current $25 carcass turn-in incentive offered by the Fish and Wildlife department.

Proponents of Sullivan's bill argue the bounty would be a welcome boost for trappers who currently rely on a weak open pelt market for compensation. Opponents argue that the bill would incentivize indiscriminate slaughter of critical species. Sources within the department have told the *News-Advertiser* that Sullivan's bill would defeat predator management efforts already under way by diverting scarce departmental funds to pay for the bounty.

Sullivan appeared briefly at yesterday's demonstration to support the hunters and outfitters, and he engaged the demonstrators directly. The leader soon dismissed his team, but he vowed he would carry their fight to the very end.

That last paragraph stuck hard in Nelson's gullet. It told every reader that Sullivan had won. He worried that other presses would pick it up, or that it might even make *The National.* He'd mapped out a precise plan to put Sullivan down that day, and he would have succeeded if only those officers and the reporter had stayed around. *He's a puny, egotistical man—all arrogance and no principle!*

He swallowed the last of his coffee and relaxed into the back of his chair. He grinned. *Well, no matter. Sullivan has no idea what'll be coming his way.*

* * * * *

The noonday sun found Minister Carson Sullivan recalling how the events of yesterday had gone just as he had wanted, except for the one thing he hadn't expected.

Sullivan's stepping stone into politics had been his job as a small-time real estate agent in Harbour Breton, a small but friendly port town on the southern tip of Newfoundland's Connaigre Peninsula. When he'd been elected to the House of Assembly, he'd become convinced that he deserved something far more prestigious than the third-generation saltbox home he'd inherited from his mother.

He'd set his mind on Sunny Cottage, the million-dollar, 1909 Queen Anne built by John Joseph Rose, the town's most successful fish merchant of the time, as an outspoken statement of his own wealth and importance. But he'd already known the current owner had no interest in selling it to him, so he'd tried to con him into selling it to a supposed unidentified buyer with a highly inflated offer. When that didn't work, he'd written letters from that same unidentified buyer impugning the owner's character and sent them to the *Harbour Breton Coastliner*. The owner had later discovered the source of those letters, and when he'd threatened a defamation lawsuit Sullivan had rapidly retreated.

Sullivan had fumed but refused to be outdone. When a large piece of land with a wide view of the barasway had come up for sale, he'd built himself an exact copy of Sunny Cottage, outfitted it with Victorian furnishings imported from London, and called it Sunny Cottage Too. *An eye for an eye*, he'd gloated at the time. No one had asked how he'd paid for it.

Now, lying comfortably on the foliate-patterned Belle de Fleur love seat in his sitting room, he grinned broadly with the memory of beating Ross Nelson at his own game yesterday, shutting down him and his pitiful team of demonstrators with the easiest of intimidations. As for Mitchell Gregg, he had long thought it was time someone gave him and his outdated department the wake-up call they deserved, and he'd been more than happy to do it.

And that reporter—*what was her name?* Emma something, he remembered the paper's editor telling him. What a perfect tool she'd turned out to be. He made a note to get copies of the photos she'd taken, especially the ones showing him gladhanding Mitchell Gregg and breaking up that ridiculous protest. They'd be great for his website and the television campaign for his predator-hunting bill. The "Law-and-Order Minister" they'd call him. He laughed out loud just thinking about it.

As for Damon Duffy, Sullivan had seen it coming. And after Duffy's performance yesterday Sullivan doubted he could count on the man for anything. That was unfortunate, but he wasn't worried. Everything Sullivan knew about Damon told him the man didn't have it in him to be a serious threat. *Weak like so many others.* He chuckled to himself.

But what Sullivan hadn't expected was Peter Joe. Sullivan remembered his father, Abraham Jeddore, a bad seed if there ever was one. He was sure Jeddore'd had a hand in killing that Harbour Breton salmon farm back in the '80s. Jeddore's people had had their own farm not far from there. Sullivan was sure Indians were no good at the fish business, so it had to have been him. And then there was the Sweet Bounty gold mine, a boon for his beloved southern Newfoundland. Sullivan was sure Jeddore had tried to kill that, too.

He was thankful Jeddore was no longer around. But the question now was, what was Peter Joe doing there yesterday? *Was he out to kill the predator bill like his no-good father would have done?* Sullivan was sure Mitchell Gregg and his department would no longer be an issue when his bill passed in the next sitting. But whatever Peter Joe was up to could only mean trouble.

He poured himself a shot of Screech to settle his mind but an old, recurring memory suddenly flared up, like a daytime nightmare. It had happened at the travelling petting zoo when he was just a boy. Young Sullivan had sat down inside the makeshift fence beside an Indian boy and had watched what the boy was doing. The boy had been sitting on the ground with his legs folded, quietly watching a coyote. He'd held out his hand and chanted something rhythmic and soft. Young Sullivan had watched the coyote move closer to him. The coyote had lain down in front of the boy, then inched forward and licked the boy's hand. The boy had turned and smiled at young Sullivan. "You try it," he'd said.

Sullivan remembered he had reached out his hand and hummed, too, but the coyote had ignored him. He'd scolded it, but still it ignored him. He'd jabbed a stick at the animal's face. The coyote had lunged at it, biting off the tip of young Sullivan's middle finger at the same time. He remembered screaming with pain as his mother had come running to snatch him up. She'd thrown a handful of dirt at the coyote and scolded the Indian boy. Then she'd hurried young Sullivan away, cursing both of them as she went.

He moaned as the missing half-digit began to throb again. He rubbed at it with the thumb of his other hand and cursed. *Indians an' coyotes, more trouble than either of them damn creatures'r worth*!

He swigged down another Screech and made his way to his Resolute executive desk. There he picked up the phone and called in a favor.

* * * * *

Damon Duffy, president of the Island Federation of Hunters and Outfitters, carried his day bag up a flight of ten stairs and passed between the six colonettes supporting the gable-end pediment of his front porch. He lived in the prestigious Rennie's Mill District, created by the wealthy residents of St. John's after the Great Fire of 1846 destroyed over two thousand downtown homes and buildings.

He strode past the Steinway grand and proceeded to his study. A Chateau Louis fireplace, one of eight in the home, crackled softly on the south wall. A fresh cup of pu-erh tea and a warm croissant, delivered minutes ago by his Bai maid of seven years, waited for him on the corner of his Felton executive desk.

He dropped his coat and day bag beside an armchair and sat down. Through the curved glass of a bow window, he stared blankly at the manicured lawn in front of his home. Despite the luxury he enjoyed every day, Damon was troubled.

He wasn't bothered by thoughts of Ross Nelson or his team of demonstrators. Nor by the reporter or the wildlife officers or the aboriginal man who'd been there with them. Not even the economy.

What occupied Damon's mind almost every day was the state of predator control in Newfoundland. What disturbed him today was the increasingly alarming behavior of its spokesperson, Assemblyman Carson "Hunter" Sullivan.

Damon was an outfitter. He'd begun with only a cook and himself as guide in a small log lodge beside Red Indian Lake. But for reasons no one could completely explain, bagging a bull moose or caribou in Newfoundland had become a bigger draw than the same trophy in almost any other province. Like other outfitters of his time, his venture had grown quickly. In his first five years he'd added four guides, two more cooks, and expanded to a fifteen-room lodge to keep up with demand. His profitability had risen dramatically. That was four years before that trio of coyotes stepped off Cape Breton onto the St. Lawrence ice bound for Newfoundland.

As a boy too young to be of help, he'd watched his father's Nova Scotia outfitting business shrivel. His father had said it was because the coyotes had come. He'd said that once they established a foothold they became impossible to stop, and the herds had dwindled in what seemed like only a few years.

When the coyotes came to Newfoundland, Damon had determined not to let the same thing happen to him or others like him. The Federation had come to life after a few fireside conversations with other outfitters who'd had the same concerns. Its mission had become to unify the voices of all island outfitters and hunters in a campaign for sensible predator control.

Sullivan was a Progressive Conservative, elected to the Assembly three years ago. At the time, he was largely unknown to that body, but that inexperience hadn't stopped him from reaching for center stage. He'd managed to get himself appointed to several influential committees, some standing, some select. It was within those committees that he'd found his path to political influence.

Sullivan's most recent appointment to the Resource Committee had put him into contact with Damon, and in that appointment Damon had found a voice in the Assembly willing to advance his cause.

But it wasn't long before Damon had learned that Sullivan had an obsession with recognition. He'd become difficult to work with, narcissistic and demanding, and he'd begun staking out extreme positions, like eradicating every last predator on the Island. His foremost skill had become demeaning anyone who spoke against him. And he'd acquired a penchant for overblowing his importance.

Sullivan had campaigned for the Assembly under his given name of Carson, and it was only after he introduced the predator-hunting bill that he began calling himself Hunter, a move Damon concluded he'd made solely to ingratiate himself with potential supporters.

Over coffee at the Jumping Bean, Damon had once suggested to Sullivan that he tone down his rhetoric. Sullivan had lashed out, accusing Damon of attacking his credibility. "Yer de one's got no damn credibility! he'd shouted, drawing stares from the other tables. "Widout me dere'd be no friggin' bill 'tall!" He'd knocked his cup off the table and stormed out scowling while pieces of the cup still skittered across the floor. No apology had been forthcoming.

Then came yesterday. *It's just like Sullivan to bring in a squad of blackguards to threaten his detractors with physical violence without telling me about it first.* Damon would never have agreed to be there if he'd thought the Federation might be associated with anything that had even the slimmest chance of ending badly.

Sullivan had become conniving, underhanded, and dangerous. Damon worried that Sullivan's behavior would tarnish both his and the Federation's credibility. And if he sullied either one, he'd threaten the future of reasonable predator control in Newfoundland.

Damon felt a chill. He strode to the Chateau Louis and squatted before the ebbing fire. He stirred the coals with a hand-wrought George III poker, threw on another log, and mulled his options as the fire's crackle returned.

6

Wildlife Intern Lucie Headley's sat at her desk in the Fish and Wildlife Department's Central District office, a brick-and-steel-clad building on Queensway in Grand Falls-Windsor. Her cubicle sat behind the third of six sets of double windows on the building's west side and looked out on an identically constructed building which housed the local offices of the Department of Education.

Her office was only a four-meter square, but it came with an oaken desk and a squeaky swivel chair that together reminded her of her family's prairie farm home, a matching two-shelf bookcase filled with the university texts she thought would be handy during her internship, and a gray, three-drawer metal filing cabinet. An old wooden coat rack she had found at the Salvation Army stood just outside her office door. A note on her to-do list reminded her to sand out the nicks, fill the cracks, and give it a fresh coat of paint.

Lucie mentally reviewed the procedures for preparing the samples she had collected yesterday. She knew the department's lab could perform some basic kinds of analyses. One of the techs in the lab had begun to autopsy the eagle carcasses and had already given Lucie the contents of each of the eagles' crops, proventriculi, and gizzards to include with her own samples. Analyses of these samples would be necessary to prove a direct link between the poisoned carcass and the eagles' deaths.

Her time at U Saskatchewan had taught her that a specialized piece of equipment would be necessary to detect the class of toxins she expected to find. The department's lab didn't have one, so she would have to deliver the samples to an offsite lab. She'd been told that all she had to do was choose one from the department's open contract, specify the class of analytes that she wanted the lab to study, package the samples, and send them off.

She found three pre-approved laboratories for the kinds of analyses she needed. She chose one at random and printed a purchase order and the following label:

Deliver to:
Sir Wilfred Grenfell College, School of Science and the Environment
20 University Drive
Corner Brook, NL   A2H 5G4
Attention: Dr. Annamarie Chartier
Enclosed FWD Purchase Order # 05-MUNGC-1
Contents: DANGEROUS GOODS

It was vital to protect the samples from heat and damage during shipping, so she covered each of them in foam wrap, transferred them to a high density polyethylene container, and covered them with dry ice. She covered the contained in a thick insulating wrap, and placed the wrapped container in a cardboard box. She placed the purchase order on top of the container, sealed the box, and attached the address label.

But this was her first time sending samples off to an offsite lab—at school, the lab was just down the hall. She soon learned that Canada Post would not ship a dangerous goods package from its office in Grand Falls-Windsor, and there were no other overnight shipping services here. Her only options were to have someone at the lab deliver it for her, or deliver it herself. She typed the address for the college into Google Maps, and quickly learned she could drive there in a little under three hours.

She stretched her arms over her head and spun her chair around. *It would be nice to see a little of western Newfoundland, maybe even squeeze in a side trip.* She'd heard a lot about the fjord of Western Brook Pond in Gros Morne National Park. She'd have to take a day off, but she had worked the previous two Saturdays and she had no pressing tasks scheduled tomorrow. She'd leave Mr. Gregg a note, but she was sure he wouldn't mind.

She plotted the route on her cell phone: drive to Norris Point today, visit Gros Morne tomorrow, deliver the samples to the Corner Brook lab first thing Thursday morning, and be back home that evening.

With the box under her arm, she grabbed her coat and backpack and dropped the note on Mr. Gregg's desk. She put everything else onto the front seat of the '85 Ford Escort that had been her parents' first car together. Her father had refurbished it as a graduation and send-off gift for his only daughter's first journey out of the province on her own.

One of her tires gave a quick squeal on the pavement as she entered Queensway. She stopped at her apartment to pack a change of clothes, then put herself onto Cromer Avenue toward its interchange with the westbound lane of the Trans-Canada Highway.

7

I turned right at Route 365's junction with the Bay d'Espoir Highway, drove another two and a half kilometers to Jipu'ji'j'kuei Kuespem Park, then made my way to the beach near the floatplane base.

Emma had called yesterday to clarify plans, and I suggested we meet here instead of the reserve. She said she'd be driving a red '95 Chevy Lumina, but it wasn't here. We had agreed on eight-thirty. She still had fifteen minutes, so I turned off the engine and waited. I hoped she wouldn't be late. We had a long way to go today and I was needed at the reserve by two o'clock. I took off my helmet, sat on the ground against a rear tire, and looked out over the long, glassy surface of Little River Pond.

Jipu'ji'j would soon close for the year and I waited alone. The air was clean, cold, and still, but the sun had already begun to warm my face. I loosened the top half of my coverall.

A small brook trout rose to sip an insect from the water's surface, sending out a single round ripple that spread and died just beyond my feet. Distant, wispy cirrus beyond the pond's southwest end hung in the sky as if fixed in place.

A loon called from the far end of the lake, a sound I have always thought both haunting and hypnotic at the same time, a sign our Spirit Creator is close, a sign this land is still wild. Some say the loon cries for its lost mate. The Old Ones tell us the Loon People cry to be with our ancient warrior and protector Kluscap to be his friends and his servants.

The loon's call faded into the surrounding hillsides and it became stone quiet again. It was as tranquil here as I've ever known it to be. I closed my eyes and let my mind drift.

Too much mystery surrounded these past weeks and I wasn't getting much help sorting things out. Today would be my first attempt to get some of those answers for myself. But exactly what I'd find when I got there I didn't know.

My father would have known what to do now, where to start, where to end. *How did he always know? Or did he? Was he just as confused at the beginning as I was now? And if he was, how did he find his way?* I wondered if I'd ever see things as clearly as he did.

The sound of tires on gravel stirred me out of my thoughts. I turned around in time to see the expected Chevy Lumina come to a halt just behind me—she was right on time.

"Hey, Chief Joe! Nice to see you again!"

I was happy to see she had dressed for the outdoors—jeans, a wool shirt, sunglasses, hiking shoes, and the Canadiens hat I had seen her in the other day. A camera hung under her arm, and a notebook protruded above her shirt pocket.

"Hello, Emma. It's nice to see you again, too."

She eyed my vehicle. "ATV. Kawasaki Brute Force, I'd say."

"Yep. Bored out for additional horsepower, four-wheel drive, custom fitted with a rear seat and knobby tires for eleven inches of ground clearance. Perfect for where we're going today."

She nodded. "Sweet machine."

"You'll need these." I dug a coverall, helmet, and gloves from a pack strapped to the front tote rack and handed them to her.

She worked herself into them and centered herself on the rear seat. "Ready to rocket!"

I started the engine and with a twist of the throttle we were on our way. At the park's entrance, I turned right onto Bay d'Espoir Highway, and almost immediately turned left onto a gravel road that would take us to a power line right-of-way.

This road was seldom used, usually only for power line maintenance, the occupants of the four homes beside it, and the few people prepared enough to take the arduous ground route into the Bay du Nord Wilderness. Most visitors would choose to be dropped by air at Kaegudeck, Koskaecodde, or Jubilee Lakes for camping, fishing, hunting, or canoeing, to be retrieved later. Others might be dropped at Medonnegonix Lake to challenge in kayaks the more than fifty rapids along the Bay du Nord River, then float the rest of it to its mouth at Yankee Cove.

To be able to use this road and the right-of-way today was a blessing, but I knew it would end long before we arrived at our destination. This country is as rugged as any land. It is at times densely covered with balsam fir, juniper, and heavy undergrowth, at times with bare and broken rock, and always with ponds, water pockets, bogs, and fens. It is knitted with streams lazy and fast, and its hills and valleys can be deceptively steep. The best routes through it change with the season. Where the road and right-of-way ended, we'd have to make our way by trial and error.

I mused that the Johns must have approached the wilderness along this same route, probably in the old Jeep

Comanche that Mickey's father owned. I wondered if we would see its tracks along our way.

The road paralleled the drainage of Little River, a series of lakes and stream linkages that emptied into Little River Pond where I had waited for Emma. We passed several homes, diverted right at the fork, and rode through a pair of shallow valleys with small streams. Where the road intersected the power line right-of-way, we passed a Newfoundland Hydro staging area. I found some level ground and stopped for a short break. I turned to face Emma as much as my seat would allow.

"How are you so far?" I asked.

"Great. How far to where we're going?"

"About twenty kilometers. You'll be on that seat for a while yet."

"Not a problem."

I pointed out our surroundings while we rested. Here, as far as we could see to the east and west, stretched a seventy-meter-wide path cleared of all but the shortest vegetation. Overhead ran two triplets of wires, each triplet strung from the outstretched arms of its own tower. Those wires originated at the Bay d'Espoir hydroelectric plant, twenty-two kilometers to our west as the eagle flies. 735,000 volts pushed the largest part of that power toward St. John's some 270 kilometers to the east. The rest of that power went north and west from the plant, lighting nearly the entire western half of the island. It was a massive electric distribution system.

All that power gave the wires a low-grade crackle, and I could feel it. Emma complained about it, too, and after she snapped a few photos we moved on.

The road continued on the high side of the right-of-way, then curved around the lower end of a lake where we crossed a bridge over the Little River itself. Where the road ended, we were forced to travel only the right-of-way. More power lines, more crackle, more land devoid of meaningful growth.

We passed over a wide, flat, hilltop splattered with large and small water pockets. Some of them flowed together to form the trickle of a new stream, while the dry summer had left others completely disconnected. They would stay that way until the snows and rains of the late fall arrived to join them all together once again.

I stopped again and looked for landmarks and prominent features to familiarize myself with this place once again. I had to be certain I could find my way back later. A small break in the trees to my right caught my attention. I dismounted and pushed my way through the underbrush to a partially overgrown roadway, heavily eroded by what seemed to have been years of rain, runoff, and disuse. I thought back to the many days I had spent with my father in this country, but no memories of it came. Emma took a few photos, and I put us back on our way.

Sometime later, we crossed a small stream and crested a broad hill. I stopped again to scan the country around us for a route. To our right lay a wide bog draining to a small lake shaped like a running dog with an oversized head. Behind us stood a steep hillside densely covered with balsam fir, juniper, and heavy undergrowth. Straight ahead lay more right-of-way, but I decided it was time for a more direct path toward our destination.

I turned to the left and chose a path down a broken rocky hillside, pushed through some light underbrush, and crossed a pair of ephemeral streambeds to another small rocky outcrop. From there, I fought our way through heavy undergrowth and up a steep hillside to its rocky crown. A bare and rocky ridge led us to another hilltop. Here I stopped to get my bearings once again.

A large, crescent-shaped pond lay between us and the steep ridge that protected the western edge of Medonnegonix , so we would have to take a less direct route to the lake's shore. Straight ahead seemed like the best choice.

That was when the sound of another ATV came to me faintly from the distance, straining as if climbing a hill. It wasn't unusual to encounter others in this area, but they were few and usually the mostly hardy, like hunters or backpackers. I wondered what part of the Bay du Nord they were scouting.

I forced the Kawasaki slowly down a steep hillside densely covered with underbrush. We had to reverse and try again several times. But when we finally broke through on the other side, my determination was rewarded with a long expanse of gently sloped, bare rock. It paralleled the lake's western ridge and extended for what I guessed to be at least three kilometers. *A stroke of luck*, I said to myself and drove on.

We were close now. The eastern shore of Medonnegonix peeked out at us beyond the hills at the east end of that valley, and just beyond it lay Koskaecodde. The lakes were joined at their northern tips, like two pears hanging from the same stem.

But dry ground was scarce, certainly not enough to drive a Kawasaki over. And the trees were closely packed. We'd surely be forced into the marshes, stalled up to our foot rests in muck and water.

To our right I noticed a small clearing where the grass looked as if it had been trampled, or maybe packed down intentionally. I dismounted and walked over to investigate. I squatted for a closer look. I ran my hand over it. It indeed had been heavily trampled, and here and there I found signs of animal droppings.

Of course. This is where Search and Rescue would have rested and grazed their horses before retrieving our Elder's body. Could this also be where the Johns had parked their Comanche? And RCMP their vehicles or horses, too? In any case, it was clear this is where we'd have to abandon the Kawasaki.

I stood and looked again over the marshy valley below, the heavily treed hillsides ahead, and the watery plateau beside us. If there was a path forward for the Kawasaki here, it was well hidden. It seemed hopeless to try. If the Johns and the RCMP had indeed parked here, they must have walked the rest of the way. I returned to the Kawasaki and killed the engine.

Emma pulled off her helmet and held it in her lap. "Is this the place?"

"Not quite," I responded. "We'll have to go the rest of the way on foot. A couple kilometers more."

She dismounted and waved her hand at the wilderness around us. "It looks pretty rugged. You're sure this is the right place?"

I pointed at the clearing. "Others have been here before us. There must be a trail nearby; we just have to find it."

We stored our helmets on our seats and searched for a trail. I began at the north side of the clearing while Emma walked to its eastern edge. Suddenly, she shrieked.

I looked over to see a bull moose lift its head and stare directly at Emma from within the brush at the edge of the clearing. Emma froze.

The bull stomped once, then again. It pinned back its ears and tossed its head. Its dead-on stare said she had no business in his territory.

"Emma! Back away slowly but don't take your eyes off it!" I began moving toward her slowly.

I came up behind her. "I'm here," I whispered. "Keep doing exactly what you're doing. I'll be right here."

We backed away together. The bull took a step forward and tossed its head again. It snorted. Then it just watched and waited, as if it were now uncertain about what to do. After another minute, it turned and bolted into the trees.

Emma wheeled around, trembling. "Shit, that was scary!"

"You did well. It shouldn't happen again; he knows we're here now and he'll avoid us."

Eventually, Emma calmed a bit and stepped back. I put my hands on her shoulders and looked her in the eye. "You okay to go on?"

"I think so."

I walked to where the moose had disappeared. On a shrub I found a long strand of coarse dark hair, and on the bare earth below it the deep imprint of a horseshoe. It wasn't a well-worn trail, but it was a trail nonetheless. I walked the first few yards of it to be sure.

"On the bright side, " I said as I returned, "your friend just showed us the way."

I went to the Kawasaki to retrieve the shoulder pack with the first aid kit and a twelve-inch Buck knife in case we had real trouble. From a side pocket, I removed a bell that I clipped to my belt loop—something to help the bull remember we were around. There'd be no signal here, so we left our cell phones behind.

I stopped for just a moment, taking in the hills and valleys surrounding us. I closed my eyes and breathed in. We were only a hundred meters higher in elevation than the parking lot where we started, but the air here seemed colder, crisper, fresher. And the sun warmer. There was something about wilderness, something bigger and grander than ourselves. I treasured this country. I took one more deep, long breath and let it out. I was ready now. Emma took a few more photos, then followed me.

The trail was gentle and flat at the beginning, but as we entered a grove of trees it became a steeper downhill slope. Where it leveled out again, we had a preview of the lakeshore through a small break in the trees. Thirty minutes later, we came out of the trees altogether into a hillside clearing looking out on the entire northern half of Medonnegonix.

"What a view!" Emma remarked. She seemed much more relaxed now, and her camera came out again.

"That it is. One of the best. This is what keeps me alive inside."

"Moose aside, you're a lucky man to have this in your world."

"Indeed I am."

I looked at my watch again. Ten-thirty. "But it's back to work now."

We soon found ourselves in another stand of mature trees on another steep slope. I stopped to look up at the trail behind us. Was this where young Mickey had run back for his father? I could not imagine what he must have been feeling then, the fear he must have held inside. I worried about him—he had hidden himself away for so long now. I wondered if he blamed himself for what had happened, as I sometimes blamed myself for my father's death. *If only I'd gone to him sooner. If only I'd known.*

We went on. We were getting close to the place Clarence had pointed out on his map. I stopped as we entered another clearing and scanned its edges for the markers Clarence had said RCMP might have left behind. At its far edge I saw the briefest flicker of yellow. That had to be it.

We crossed the clearing and stepped into a ring of yellow tape. 'Police Line Do Not Cross' it said, and it enclosed an area about thirty meters across. Stakes and other markers pointed out things that probably were of interest to RCMP but made no sense to me.

For a moment, I hesitated— the RCMP should already have collected any evidence it found. But my gut told me that they had to have missed something—the thing that connected Leon, the eagles, and Armless Man, the thing I was looking for.

"Is this it? The place where Leon John died?" Emma asked.

"Yes, it seems so."

"Great. So, what are we looking for?"

"I'm not entirely sure. Signs of a struggle? Something that doesn't look right? Anything out of the ordinary, I think. Just keep your eyes open."

Side-by-side, we scoured the area in rows from one end to the other, sometimes on foot, sometimes on hands and knees. We moved dead branches. We swept the grass with our feet, turning it over and back again. We reversed our path and scoured again until we had covered every inch of the clearing twice. We found nothing.

I stepped over the tape and sat down on a log at the edge of the clearing. I was frustrated. I began to wonder if Clarence, the coroner, and RCMP had been right after all. Maybe I should have taken Clarence's advice and just left it all alone. I felt suddenly foolish.

Emma sat down beside me. She looked tired. Surely she was frustrated to find not even a shred of a story here. She took a deep breath and huffed it out. Neither of us said a word for a long time. She took another breath, then broke the silence.

"What's that smell?"

"What smell?"

"I'm not sure. Rotted meat?"

I smelled only fir and spruce. "Where?"

"I don't know. But it's close." She looked to her right and sniffed. She looked to her left and sniffed again.

"Very close," she said. We both stood and searched.

She followed the smell into the trees while I tagged closely behind. Now I began to smell it, too. A few steps later, Emma stopped and looked at me in bewilderment. She pinched her nose closed and pointed at the ground. "What the hell is that?"

I stooped. "It's a carcass and entrails."

"Carcass and entrails?"

"Animal bones and guts. Looks like coyote. My guess is . . . "

"Oh, gawd!" She nearly gagged as she walked back toward the log. I followed, and that's when my eye suddenly caught something unusual. I had nearly stepped on it. It was only ten meters from the end of our log. I squatted to get a better look. It was attached to something in the ground. There was a distinct odor here, too, but this time it smelled like fish.

"What's that?" she asked.

I stood and walked to its other side. "I have no idea. But it's certainly unusual. Can you get a photo, and the surroundings, too?"

She captured several photos of it and everything around us. I knelt down and slowly dug around it, careful to keep my face away just in case. It loosened, and I eased it out of its hole. I was looking at a small cylinder wrapped in a narrow strip of red cloth attached to the top of a tubular metal stake. She squatted to study it with me.

"Could this be what your caller's son found?" I asked.

She took a few close ups. "I'd say it has all the right pieces."

"I think you're right."

If this was what I thought it was, I had to assume it was live and store it well. I dug through my pack and pulled out a rag and the plastic first aid kit. I emptied the kit into the pack, and wrapped the device in gauze and the rag. The wrapped device fit snugly into the kit. I snapped it shut, cushioned it all around in a spare shirt, and stowed it in the pack.

"I can't believe RCMP missed this. "Let's get your photos to Mitchell, and RCMP, too. Maybe one of them knows—"

Something cracked in the air and ripped at the leaves beside me. Then came the boom of a high-powered rifle.

"Get DOWN, NOW!" I yelled. The rifle's echo bounced off the hills around us. We dropped to the ground and crawled up close behind the log. We huddled there in fear. *Was it a stray? Were we the target?*

The answer came too quickly. The second bullet cracked over the top of the log and tore into the dirt only a meter or two beyond our feet. We dug in closer while the second report and its echo told me just how vulnerable we were.

"What the hell?" Emma cried out, cringing.

I put my finger to my lips. "I don't know," I whispered. "But I'd say somebody doesn't want us here. Stay quiet and stay down."

We were deep in the hills and it suddenly struck me that my insistence of finding what killed our Elder might just get us killed, too, though maybe not in the same way.

A third bullet cracked, skinned our log, and ricocheted into a tree behind us. I quickly looked at my watch. One second ... two seconds, then the report, then the echo off the north hills.

Two seconds . . . three hundred meters a second . . . a little more than half a kilometer away. Probably somewhere in the west hills, surely using a scope, and hopefully using a bolt action. Reload, re-aim, squeeze off the shot . . . about nine seconds total if we were lucky.

"Change of plans, Emma. After the next one we're going to run like hell up the trail and into the trees on the other side of this clearing."

"What? Are you nuts?"

"Maybe. But we're ducks on a pond here. We need something between him and us, and trees are all we've got. Stay low and run like you've never run before."

"Damn. You're one crazy . . . "

Another crack, then a dull smack shook our log.

"Jesus!" she yelped.

"NOW, Emma! GO!"

We jumped up . . . *one* . . . bolted through the tape . . . *two* . . . the report came . . . *three* . . . we were into the clearing . . . *four . . . the bell!* I ripped it off my hip and cupped it in my hand . . . *five . . . six . . . was that thing in the pack safe? . . . seven* . . . we're getting closer . . . *eight . . . nine* . . . we ran into the trees, hit the ground, and covered our heads.

I counted ten . . . twenty . . . thirty seconds. Silence. I raised up my head and listened again. An engine revved in the distance. It grew louder, then faded.

I rose to my knees. "I think he's gone."

She stayed close to the ground. "Are you sure?"

"As sure as I can be from here. That sound? I think it was him driving away."

She relaxed somewhat and sat up. "So now what?"

"Well, I think we should get out of here, now."

"Ditto. Let's get the holy shit away from this place."

We rose to our feet and ran up the trail toward the Kawasaki. At the view of Medonnegonix, we stopped to catch our breath and rest our aching sides and thighs, crouching on the ground to avoid being seen. I listened hard for that ATV, wondering if he'd be tracking us, and thought again about how far we were from help.

But we had to go on, and we resumed our uphill run. Another fifteen minutes put us out of the last grove of trees and into the meadow. There, thankfully, still stood the Kawasaki—no flat tires, no bullet holes in the gas tank. We sweated inside the coveralls but we both started to relax. I stowed the bell in my pack and strapped it to the front tote rack. We took only a minute to catch our breath again, then pulled on our helmets and straddled our seats.

"Hang on," I called back to Emma. I turned the Kawasaki around and cranked it. Tree and brush covered hillsides, marshes and stream crossings, and rocky ridges flew past us, all in reverse order, and as fast as I could make the Kawasaki go.

A grueling half hour later, I stopped where we first had left the right-of-way, across from the old abandoned road. I turned off the engine and removed my helmet. I scanned the hillsides and listened for any sign that we'd been followed. It seemed clear enough for a short break.

My body still quivered, as if it were still bouncing over rocks and streams and trail. And I'd ridden on the back seat of one of these ATVs often enough to wonder if Emma felt like Jell-O.

"I think we're okay here for a while," I said. "But we shouldn't stay long."

"Back in a minute," she said, removing her helmet. We climbed off the Kawasaki and set our helmets on the seat. She walked off "to get the feeling back in my legs" she'd said, while I bent from the waist to relax my back and get the blood flowing to my head again.

A mosquito buzzed my ear. I'd already swatted at it when it hit me that this was September, already too cold for mosquitos. I stood upright. It was the whine of an ATV. It was coming from where we had just been, and it was coming fast.

Now Emma heard it, too, and she bolted back. "Is that the same bastard I think it is?"

We threw our helmets on and jumped onto our seats. "Hang on, Emma!" I twisted the throttle hard and rocketed to the abandoned road. We plowed through the brush and bounced over ruts. I swung a hard left. We ducked our heads and drove deep into the trees. I killed the engine. We held our breath. We waited.

The sound grew louder, racing, then straining, then racing again. He was closing on us at a high rate of speed. *Had he followed us through the hills? Did he know this road?* I prayed he didn't.

He was nearly on top of us now. I was certain he'd see the broken brush, our tracks. He'd stop. He'd find us.

Then the sound began to fade. A plume of dust wafted over our heads. Eventually, the sound died out altogether. I craned my neck to see through the trees and listened. Nothing.

We looked at each other and sighed audibly at the same time. Her face told me we were both thinking that for the second time today we were lucky to be alive. I took a deep breath. I was about to ask again if she was okay, but she rolled her eyes as if to say my question would have been foolish.

I had no idea where the abandoned road went, but it had to be safer than the way our pursuer had gone. It promised a long, steep climb to the top of a hill, maybe eighty meters higher than where we sat right now. But no more than ten meters up, it became barren rock. And it was completely clear from there all the way to the top. *How could I not have known about this?*

For ten long minutes the Kawasaki groaned as we climbed. At the top of the slope, I stopped to once again look at the path ahead. I saw a long barren ridge that led to yet another ridge that didn't end until it dipped into Hermitage Bay, well south of us and well beyond my own Reserve. We had an uninterrupted view that stretched for what I guessed to be forty kilometers or more, all the way to Cabot Strait.

"Damn, what a view!" Emma pointed at the horizon. "That's the ocean, right?"

We had a heart stopping view of my ancestors' homelands. They must have loved that this was home, just as I was honored to call it my own home. It reminded me how fortunate I was to have been drawn back to this land, despite the reason why.

"Magnificent, isn't it."

We sat there mesmerized for almost five minutes before the reason we were here reminded me that we still had a long way to go.

The next kilometer or two on the first ridge were flat and easy, then the downhill slope steepened and we had to slow. We muddled our way through a pair of shallow water pockets, then rose back up onto solid rock. Twenty minutes later, the bottom of our ridge led us back into the trees.

Here our path was no more than a narrow, rutted trail once again. We lumbered along, dodging ruts where we could, letting them carry us down the hill where we couldn't. A few minutes later, it dead-ended at a dry streambed running across our path. On the other side of it stood a dense growth of brush and trees. I could see no way through.

I killed the engine and put my helmet on my seat. Emma stayed behind while I walked the streambed to the left, searching for a way through the growth. Rocks and exposed roots hidden by the brush that had grown up around them grabbed at my boots.

I turned and walked it in the other direction. A short distance beyond the Kawasaki, I found what appeared to be a small gap. It was barely half my body's width. I put my arms in front of my face and pushed myself into it. Branches clawed at my coverall and scraped my hands, and I could not see even my own feet. But when I broke through, I found myself standing beside a paved road. I pushed myself back through the gap and returned to Emma and the Kawasaki.

"You won't believe this, Emma, but we're about forty meters from civilized travel." I pointed my thumb over my shoulder. "And Jipu'ji'j is only a couple kilometers that way. All we have to do is figure out how to get there. The stuff in front of us is way too dense."

She looked behind, then left, then right. "From where I sit, that could be the Trans-Canada Highway," she said, pointing at the streambed. It would be tedious and slow, but it seemed like our only choice.

"You're up for this, right? And gloves on?" I asked.

She raised up her hands, and I turned us upstream.

Branches scraped our arms and yanked at the Kawasaki's handlebar. We ducked below branches spanning the streambed. Emma dismounted and bent others upward while I lowered my head and squeezed the Kawasaki underneath. We rolled large rocks to the edge of the bed. She pushed while I groaned the Kawasaki over a flat boulder that wouldn't be moved. At one point, I duck-walked beside the Kawasaki with my hands on the grips to ease it under a pair of heavy limbs spanning from opposite sides of the bed while Emma followed on hands and knees. We crept along the streambed for what felt like an hour.

But then it abruptly ended, and I drove the Kawasaki up a small embankment onto a gravel road, the very one we had begun on this morning. And just as I expected, the Bay d'Espoir Highway ran only a few tens of meters to our left. In two minutes we were back at Jipu'ji'j.

I parked next to Emma's car and we pulled off our helmets. The look on Emma's face told me she was completely exhausted. I was certain I would hear that she never would have asked to go along today if she'd had any idea of what to expect.

"Well," she began, "today was certainly something to write home about. The part I liked best was dodging the bullets. A first for me."

We laughed. She smiled and extended her hand. Her gaze and grip lingered for what seemed like minutes. "Thanks for taking care of me today," she said finally.

"My pleasure."

She pulled back her hand. "I'll send those photos off to Mitchell Gregg and the RCMP," she added, dusting herself off.

At that, she went to her car while I strapped her coverall and helmet to the Kawasaki's front rack. I watched as she waived and drove off. What had happened today reminded me of Annamarie Chartier and the near death undertaking we'd found ourselves in nearly a year ago, trying to learn how my father had died. That was the last time we'd been together, and a subtle emptiness swept over me as I thought about that. *Should I call her? Would she remember me?*

I mounted the Kawasaki for what I hoped would be the last time today. My mind quickly replayed the day and I shook my head in disbelief. I would tell Clarence Paul about it when I returned, but would he believe it?

I donned my helmet and started the engine. My watch told me it was two-fifteen. I would be late, but maybe not too late.

8

It was nine o'clock in the morning when a taxicab dropped MHA Carson "Hunter" Sullivan in front of an old two-story building at 90 Military Road in St. John's. He walked the path of stone tiles to the limestone steps spanning the width of the building's portico. His eyes followed the middle two of its six Tuscan columns upward to their Ionic volutes. At the triangular pediment above them he found the British Royal Coat of Arms—the lions of England in the first and third quarters, the lion of Scotland in the second, and the harp of Ireland in the fourth, supported at its sides by the lion of England and the unicorn of Scotland, all in hand-carved stone relief.

But the scroll below it was where his eyes lingered. "Dieu et mon droit," he read. *God and my divine right*. He felt the inspiration of those words grow within him. His chest puffed and he grinned broadly. He congratulated himself for having chosen the Colonial Building, the 1850 cut-stone structure built as the first official House of Assembly for what had then been Britain's Colony of Newfoundland. In a few minutes, he would ply the power vested in him as a Minister of today's House of Assembly just as eloquently as Joey Smallwood had promoted confederation with Canada in January of 1948. He swelled with pride.

His eyes returned downward as he climbed the center aisle of steps. He passed between the middle two columns, took the knobs of the maroon double doors into his fists, and pushed the doors open wide. The Great Hall greeted him with its grandeur.

Inside, a team of employees conducted the business of the Department of Tourism, for by 1960 the Assembly had outgrown this building and had moved into the Confederation Building on Prince Phillip Drive. An elderly custodian noticed the doors had been left open and interrupted his cleaning round to close them.

He stepped onto the Grand Staircase and climbed its worn wooden treads, allowing his hand to feel the time-rubbed furrows in its railing. At his twelfth step, he stopped on the landing to admire the multi-colored ceiling frescoes, magnificently hand-stenciled and inlaid with two hundred books of gold leaf by Polish immigrant Alexander Pindikowski.

He returned down the staircase and turned left to face the heavy wooden doors of the honored former chamber of the House of Assembly. He glanced at his watch. Nine-fifteen. Strategically late was his phrase for it, letting the anticipation build in his audience. He snugged his red bow tie, tugged his checkered flannel suitcoat downward, and straightened its lapels. He took the knobs of the Chamber's double door in his hands. He could hear the murmur of voices behind it. This was his moment. He flung the doors open and swaggered in.

The murmur subsided as he strolled between the center two of the four columns comprising the Chamber's entrance. On a small table beside the column to his right sat the open box of envelopes his aide had delivered to this room earlier today.

He continued down the center aisle toward the far wall where a lectern, framed from above by the Coat of Arms and flanked by the two northeast windows, awaited his arrival. Above it hung a dimly lit, milk glass chandelier.

He stepped up onto the stool behind the lectern and faced his audience. He stood proudly in the very place where many before him had been addressed as Honorable Mr. Speaker. The sun illuminated him from behind through frayed and translucent roller blinds with an almost celestial glow, as if God himself had come to endorse him.

He removed his notes from an inside breast pocket and gently cleared his throat. He slowly scanned his audience from left to right, then left again.

They had all come. Hunters and trappers, sheep ranchers and poultry farmers. Tourism lobbyists, big game outfitters, and owners of emerging dairy and mink farms. Ministers of Progressive Conservative districts. About thirty people altogether, and every one of them someone he'd given personal influence during his time in the Assembly. And as he'd so carefully planned, not a single member of the press.

He waited until all eyes were fixed on him alone. Then, he spoke. 'Mornin', b'ys. Mornin', ladies." He paused briefly.

"Dear friends. You are the people that know too well our beloved province is de victim of an historic invasion. Dey came without warning in '85, when we knew nothing about 'em. Dey took over everything. Dey have no enemies. Dey spread disease and parasites wherever dey go."

His voice grew more intense. "Dey kill your sheep, your lambs, your calves, your caribou an' moose! Dey steal your hunter's trophies, plunge farmers and ranchers into bankruptcy! Dey're conniving, sneaky, an' ruthless! Dey obey no law but their own thirst for blood an' flesh!"

He lowered his voice. "And soon—" he paused for effect "—dey'll overrun your cities and towns. Your children will not be safe. Dey'll no longer play at their schools, in their neighborhood streets, or even in their own backyards. Dese invaders'll kill your dogs and cats. Your family pets will live only in your memories."

His voice rose. "You know what I'm talkin' about, eh? You've seen them stalking your ranches, your hunting grounds, your farms, your yards. Dey cripple your livelihoods, your way of life, and dare I say threaten your very presence on de Rock itself!

He calmed his voice again. "Yes, I'm talking about coyotes and wolves. Varmints. Useless miscreants worse than skunks that our misguided bureaucrats only wanna study. Beasts that their radical, liberal advocates say are de victims of mankind." He exaggerated a snicker and drew a few smirks from the front row.

His voice rose an octave. "But dey are assassins! And dey are butchers! And we must stop them in their very tracks! Dey deserve everything we can do to get rid of them!"

He paused, letting the echo drive his words home. A few shouts of "Aye!" arose within his audience, and he nodded toward them. Then he lowered his voice yet again.

"I came to your aid with a bill to annihilate this menace at its roots. I will continue this good work into de next Assembly, and into de next one, if necessary. As long as it takes to eliminate every vestige of dis plague."

"All I ask is that you support me as you have in the past, and I in return pledge to support you as I always have. Together we can restore our livelihoods, restore safety for our children and families." His voice rose again. "And make de Rock what it once was—strong, secure, and free!"

Shouts of agreement rained down from all corners of the room. He let them linger before beginning again.

"In 1949, here within this very hallowed room, Newfoundlanders with all kinds of political views came together to create on dis island a new, free, and prosperous land. To shed the shackles of Britain heavy upon deir wrists. And dey succeeded magnificently, eh? Today, because of what dey did so many years ago, we thrive hand-in-hand with our new mother, Canada."

"Hear hear!" rang out from around the room. He let the cheers die down before continuing.

"Yes, my friends, yes!" He nodded to emphasize his agreement. "And I'm here to dissolve dese new shackles heavy on your wrists. To give you a freedom reborn, a freedom of safety and prosperity once again. And we shall succeed as magnificently as dose before us did in dis very room in 1949. Are you with me?" he shouted. He thrust his fist upward and shouted again, "Are you with me?"

A wave of applause swept the room, and raised fists sprang up. He allowed the audience to revel in its agitation, and he basked in his moment of glory. When the energy at last subsided, he motioned for them to quiet.

"You're too kind, my friends, thank you," he resumed. "And now I ask a favor. Lobby your friends and family, your neighbors, your clients and customers, your city administrators, and your Ministers. Spread de word that a new Newfoundland is coming. Urge 'em to support me in dis just and righteous cause. That is my single and humble request. You will not regret it, I promise!"

"Hear hear!" arose again. He letr the audience settle.

"And now I must go to resume dis important work. As my appreciation for coming here today"—he pointed toward the table at the Chamber's entrance—"please take an envelope on your way out."

The audience rose in raucous applause. He reached out for them with open hands and a grand smile. Stepping off the stool, he thrust the two-fingered V of victory into the air with both hands. The crowd flowed toward him. He moved among them with the ease of someone who had orchestrated moments like this before, pumping hands and thanking them profusely as he went from one to the other. Triumph beamed from his face.

* * * * *

Damon Duffy rose unnoticed from his seat in the corner under the balcony. He walked behind the last row of chairs toward the exit, then stopped beside the table with the open box. He removed one of the envelopes and squeezed its contents with one hand while his other hand quickly counted the envelopes still in the box. About sixty, he estimated.

He slid a finger under the envelope's lightly sealed flap, pulled it back, and spread the envelope open. Inside, he found Sullivan's official calling card and a two-hundred-fifty-dollar Visa gift card. He pushed the contents back inside, closed the flap, and returned the envelope to the box.

He stood for a few moments with arms folded and watched Sullivan glad-hand the crowd. He shook his head in disgust. "Unbelievable," he muttered.

Outside the Colonial Building, he walked down the limestone steps and turned left to the parking lot where his restored Mercedes SL waited. He leaned against a front fender, pulled a cell phone from the inside pocket of his navy blue sport coat, and dialed. He loosened the gray knot of his necktie as he waited. Three rings later, the man on the other end of that call picked up.

"Hello, Damon," the man said.

"Evan, things have gone too far, as we expected they would. It's time. Battery Café, tomorrow, nine-thirty."

"You got it, Damon. We'll be there."

9

I turned into the rear parking lot of the administration building and guided the Kawasaki into its marked space. It was two thirty-five and I was already more than half an hour late. I would not make a good impression today.

I loaded my arms with the packs and my helmet and hastened to the back entrance. I pushed at the handicap switch with my elbow and walked through as it swung open. The stairway and floor creaked as I double-timed them to my corner office on the second floor.

Dumping the packs and helmet onto the floor in a corner behind the door, I gently shook my backpack off my shoulders into my side chair. I stripped off my coverall and hurried out of the building to the powwow grounds. A clear sky with a warm sun and a cool, crisp breeze greeted me on the way. It would be a good day for a ceremony.

The powwow grounds sat on a broad and grassy hilltop with a grand view to the west and south. I crossed them and turned into the trees along a narrow footpath. At the end of that footpath, in the center of a clearing, about fifteen of my people stood together in a makeshift circle. To the left of their circle was a low, dome-shaped lodge with a fire burning a few meters in front of its entrance. What I saw told me I wasn't late after all. I breathed a sigh of relief.

This was where those troubled by the events of the past few weeks, or by any other burden over the past months or even years, would have an opportunity to grieve, sing, talk, pray, and receive support in one of our most private ceremonies—a sweat.

Conductor Jason Sam was speaking to the participants as I arrived. I waited out of view behind a cluster of birch to avoid diverting their attention from him. When he finished his instructions, I emerged.

"Pjila'si, Saqamaw," he said as I joined the circle.

"Pjila'si, Jason. And pjila'si to all of you today."

I scanned the circle slowly, wanting to reach each participant. Some I knew had sweated before, and I recognized their comfort with this ritual. Others would be sweating for their first time today. Although Jason had familiarized them at length with what they were about to experience, I still saw apprehension in their eyes. It was to them that I spoke.

"I remember my own first sweat," I began, gently singling out each of them with my eyes. "I was a few years younger than the youngest of you here. And as my conductor spoke to me just as Jason did to you today, try though he did to put me at ease, I can tell you that there was only one thing on my mind." I paused. "Fear."

A round of laughter arose among them, and I met it with a broad grin. I knew then that I had reached them.

"What was I afraid of? I was afraid I would learn something about myself that I didn't want to know, or that I would offend someone, or even offend the tradition of the sweat itself. But inside the lodge, I came to a deeper understanding of myself and my place among our people. The outside voices—those truly outside our community and those voices in my head that created doubt and insecurity within me—were gone. I found a deeper connection to our grandfathers and grandmothers, to my family, and to my community.

"My conductor then was Jason's father, so you can do no better than to trust his guidance and wisdom completely.

"There are two more things you should know. First, each of you will hold a special place in our people's spiritual history today. Some of you may know that we haven't always been able to perform our sacred rituals as you are about to do now. Slowly over two centuries, driven by intimidation, assimilation, and the scorn of missionaries, the sweat, like many of our spiritual practices, was taken from us. Our Old Ones were forced to give up these practices. They had become so unfamiliar that we turned to our brothers the Sioux and the Lakota for help in relearning them. By simply being here today, you are helping our people relive our true native heritage. And for this you can be proud. You are Mi'kmaq.

"And second, remember that you do this not just for yourself, but for your family, your friends, and for all our people. That is why we begin and end with the words 'Msit No'kmaq,' 'All My Relations.' It reminds us that we are all connected. When you heal here"—I held the flat of my fist to my heart—"you heal those around you, too."

I saw heads lift up and nod. "You have nothing to fear and so much to gain," I ended.

"Wela'lin, Saqamaw," they replied in unison.

With that, I turned and walked back along the footpath that had brought me here. They were in good hands now, and I knew they would grow from their experience.

The footpath opened onto the powwow grounds and I once again felt the warm sun and soft breeze on my face. I stood for a moment, taking it all in again. But too soon the responsibility of my office called and I went on.

Back at my desk, a glance at the phone told me I had two messages. I dialed for voice mail and listened.

The first message had come this morning and offered me three days at a St. John's hotel at a never-before-heard-of rate. I deleted it.

The second was from Mitchell Gregg, received just ten minutes ago. He'd ended with "Call me when you get this," and there was urgency in his voice. I dialed his number.

He answered immediately. "Chief?"

"Mitchell? Yes, it's me. I heard your message, what's—"

"Emma sent me those photos she took this morning. You still have that thing?"

I glanced at the backpack on the chair beside my desk. "I do. It's padded inside a first aid kit box."

"Good, but it wouldn't hurt to pad its some more. So find a box. Line it with cotton, crumpled newspaper, anything like that. Gently put that thing inside and cover it with more of the same stuff. Close the box, take it outside, put it where no one'll stumble onto it. Then call me back."

"What is it, Mitchell?" I asked.

"Explain later. Sooner you do that the better."

"Okay. I'll call you back in a few minutes."

"I'll be waitin'," he said and hung up.

I wondered why he was being so secretive, but I wasted no time getting to the basement storeroom. In the far corner behind a pair of work boots and a shovel, I found a box that looked to be about the right size. I emptied it onto a shelf, grabbed a handful of cleaning rags from the shelf below, and hustled back up the stairs to my office.

I crumpled three of the rags into the bottom of the box. I carefully removed the first aid kit box with the device still inside it from my backpack and laid it gently on the rags, carefully laid the remaining rags on top of it, then closed the box. I carried the box delicately down the stairs, backed into the door's crash bar, and went outside to the parking lot.

I looked around. The gravel and grass of the parking lot didn't provide anything even remotely like a hiding place, and the urgency in Mitchell's voice told me I shouldn't leave it far from my sight. But I remembered watching from my office window as a pair of red foxes had made their winter den in a deadfall just beyond the parking lot. They and their pups had abandoned the den in July and I knew it wouldn't be used again until December.

I dropped to my hands and knees and peered inside. I dragged out a few handfuls of leaves and pine cones, and was relieved to see no sign that another animal had taken up residence. The box fit with a little room to spare, and I decided it would be safe enough there until I found a better place. I pushed in a handful of dead leaves, and went back to my office to call Mitchell.

"How'd it go?" he answered without a greeting.

"Well, I think. It's padded in a box and outside in an abandoned fox den where I can keep an eye on it. It should be okay there for now," I answered.

"Good. Best to have it away from people and animals."

"So what is that thing?" I asked.

"Looks to me like what they call a coyote getter, sometimes an M44 or cyanide bomb. Meant to keep coyotes from gettin' too close to sheep or calves. Once in a while somebody's dog'll find one and, well, that's the end of 'im."

"The end of him?"

"Yeah. That little cylinder on top? Packed with cyanide powder, an' a scented bait's wrapped around it. Coyote bites at the bait, and a spring underneath ejects the powder into its mouth. Dies in 'bout half an hour. Where'd you find it?"

"Where Leon John's body was found, up beside Medonnegonix."

"Medonnegonix? Not on private land, eh? Private land runs nearby."

"No, I know that country. We were about a hundred meters from the shore at the north end, right where Leon John was when he died."

"That's inside Bay du Nord Reserve, all right. But no reason for that kind of thing to be there."

I paused for a moment, thinking. "Tell me, Mitchell, could a device like that kill a man?" I asked.

"Kill a man? Don't think so. Not enough ten—I mean cyanide—to kill somethin' large as a man. Could cause a whole lot of pain and discomfort, though, an' could be really serious if a kid got into one."

"Got it. One more question. Why would someone shoot at us after we found it?"

"Shoot at you? Did I hear right?" he asked.

"You did. With a high-powered rifle."

"Good God, Chief. Not strays, eh, like somebody target practicin'?"

"Not unless we were the target. Four shots, all within a meter or closer to us. We were lucky to get out of there."

"Dunno, Chief. Sounds like someone really didn't want you there. Shouldn't be happenin', Bay du Nord or not."

"So what do I do now, Mitchell?"

"Don't know what to tell you, except I'd stay away from the Bay du Nord. And keep that getter where it can't do any harm. Be down your way sooner or later, an' I'll take it off your hands."

"Thanks, Mitchell. It'll be here. Let me know when you're coming."

"Will do, Chief." There was a pause in his voice, then he added, "An' be careful, right? This may be bigger than either of us know."

"Meaning?"

"I can't tell you." Then he hung up.

I was dumbstruck. This suddenly didn't sound like the Mitchell I knew.

I walked to my window with my hands in my pockets and stared emptily at the trees across the mouth of the Conifer. Nothing made sense. A cattle and sheep rancher's device staked in a place with no cattle or sheep. Emma and I almost killed after finding something that couldn't kill a man in the same place where Leon was killed. Four eagles died from . . . from what? How did Armless Man fit in?

And, if that wasn't already enough, there was now something about Mitchell that troubled me deeply.

10

At nine thirty a.m., Damon Duffy entered the Battery Café. He walked in and approached a table by the front window where two men awaiting his arrival sat looking out on Duckworth Street. He hung his wool topcoat on the back of an empty chair and sat down.

"Mornin', Evan, Jake. Good to see you both," he said with a nod.

Damon signaled for a server. "Black coffee, please," he said when she arrived. "One for each of these gentlemen, too, and an extra cup."

"Got it. And a handful of creams, just in case," she said as she left.

When the server was out of range, Damon sat forward, folded his arms, and leaned his elbows onto the table.

"Here's where we are," he said in a subdued tone. "Yesterday, Sullivan made an appeal to about fifty exclusive supporters in the old Colonial Building. Farmers, ranchers, a few of our outfitters, a couple lobbyists, and a handful of MHAs he knows he can count on. Notably, no one from the press.

"You all know his style—obnoxious and grandiose. But it was all legitimate until he directed them to a box of envelopes by the door. Inside? Altogether about fifteen thousand in gift cards, maybe more. We need to know where he's getting that kind of money.

"I think we also have to face head on what we're up against. Sullivan is in this for what he thinks he can get for himself. Favors, power, reelection, who really knows? But he's gone too far, and his bad name is rubbing off onto us. I don't think enough of the Assembly will support an all-out slaughter, which means any prospect for sensible predator control coming out of the next Assembly is dead. Which means the livelihoods of our members are on the casualty list for at least another year." He scanned the faces of his friends.

"But I'm determined we take the long view," he resumed. "We have to find someone to champion a bill that does what we want it to do. But we have to sideline Sullivan first, and we have to do it now." He stopped and looked at the others.

"As always, Damon, we're in. But how?" Evan asked.

Damon clasped his hands behind his head. His face said he wanted to hear more.

Jake spoke up. "I agree with Evan. But Sullivan'll deny anything we put out there. If we're gonna throw shit at the wall, it's gotta stick."

The shop bell jingled again and Damon looked up. A man in a gray down vest carrying a zippered pouch under his arm stopped and looked around. Damon waved and the man approached their table. Evan and Jake stared at Damon in surprise.

"Evan, Jake, say hello to Roger."

Evan leaned forward. "Do we know you, Roger?" His tone said this was the wrong time for a stranger.

"You don't," Damon interrupted. "But I think you'll appreciate what he has to say."

The server arrived just then with coffee, a bowl of creamers, and the promised extra cup. They waited until each man's cup had been filled, the pot was on the table, and the server had gone.

Roger moved the creamers and the pot aside. He unzipped his pouch, removed a folder of papers and spread them onto the table.

"Gentlemen, I give you copies of records from the Assembly's Management Commission for the past three fiscal years, the same period the member of your concern has held office. You may want to study them closely. The commission is sometimes reluctant to incriminate a member without the prospect of public support. Perhaps you will be the public it is waiting for."

He paused while the three men tried to take in what lay on the table before them.

"A few more things," he continued. "One, you must make a formal Access to Information Request for official copies of these documents. Otherwise, the commission will know you have someone on the inside and any case against said member will be suspect. Two, this is only a starter. You'll need records from Elections, Finance, and Canada Revenue. Three, I can be reached for assistance if you wish, but only through Damon. I'm sure you'll understand why. And four, if you were to call the commission directly, you'd learn that no one by the name of Roger works there."

He stood with the empty pouch in his hand. "And with that, gentlemen, I leave you." He nodded and walked to the door.

When he'd gone, Evan and Jake turned to Damon simultaneously.

"Who the hell was that guy?" Evan demanded.

"A friend of a friend. Looks like we have work to do," was all Damon said in return.

11

Lucie Headley had just disembarked today's morning tour of Western Brook Pond in Gros Morne National Park. On the three-mile walk back to her car on wooden boardwalk over the peat bogs and on graveled trail through the tuckamore, the Fish and Wildlife intern reflected on what she had seen. She scrolled through the photos on her cell phone. Glassy landscapes of crystal-blue fresh water. Sheer walls of igneous rock towering overhead. Hanging valleys ending in midair. A rare flock of cliff-nesting gulls. And high waterfalls evaporating into horsetails of mist long before reaching the water below. She was captivated by the entire tour.

She decided that the view of the water and cliffs she'd snapped at the start of the tour and her selfie with Pissing Mare Falls in the background would be good ones to send to her parents in Saskatoon. She stopped beside Jerry's Pond, chose Message, and selected her mother's phone number. She typed "It's so beautiful here!" then clicked Send and waited for the *zoo-wip* that would tell her the message was on its way. "Signal strength low" popped onto her screen instead, and she sighed. *No matter*. She could try again from Corner Brook later today. She stuffed her cell phone into her backpack and resumed the walk to her car.

At the parking lot, she threw her backpack on the floor and her coat on top of the box of samples sitting on the passenger seat, then started the engine.

The road map from her glove box told her that she could follow Provincial Route 430 along the coast back to where she yesterday had left the Trans-Canada Highway—the TCH as it was called—then take the westbound interchange at Deer Lake. The Corner Brook interchange looked more complicated, but she decided she could figure that out when she got there. And she could ask someone for motel recommendations and where to find the Grenfell lab to deliver her samples on Thursday, too.

She smiled at that thought as she shifted into reverse. She'd found people in this province to be very friendly, and asking anyone for directions usually led to hearing a lot about where she was, what had happened there, and lots of other things. Sometimes they'd even invite her for coffee.

She backed out of her spot and drove to the exit where she waited for three cars to clear her path. A hard left put her onto Route 430 toward Rocky Harbour and Deer Lake.

She took time to enjoy the expansive coastline, and to photograph the vistas and little villages along it. She stopped in Rocky Harbor for gas and postcards, took some shots of Bonne Bay Big Pond at Jackladder, then was back on the road to Deer Lake.

She stopped briefly to leave a voice message for Mitchell Gregg, then took the westbound interchange, and drove the long, flat stretch of the TCH beside the town's namesake water body for the first twenty-seven kilometers to Corner Brook. At Steady Brook, she turned left after descending the exit ramp and passed under the TCH for a short break. That's when she noticed a sign for the

Newfoundland and Labrador Heritage Tree. She parked only meters from it beside another car.

The marker told her it was a seventeen-meter-tall pole carved from a 360-year-old cedar tree, weighed nine tons, and came from Gold River, British Columbia. Its carvings represented over a thousand years of Newfoundland and Labrador history. On it she saw Vikings, Innu, Beothuk, Captain Cook, salmon, miners' tools, seals, lighthouses, factory workers, Joey Smallwood, Sir Wilfred Grenfell, icebergs, the RCMP, whales, and more.

She backed away and admired it from the roadside. As far as she knew, nothing like this could be found in Saskatoon or anywhere in Saskatchewan. She snapped photo after photo, wanting to capture each carving. She was awed by everything about it, even the lush Marble Mountain ski hill behind it. And she knew her parents would love it, too. She couldn't wait to hear their reaction when she called them from a Corner Brook motel tonight.

Satisfied she had enough photos, she returned to her car and proceeded toward the TCH. She slowed for a hunched man in tattered clothes standing on the corner in front of a shopping cart filled with plastic bags of clothes and other belongings. One hand held out a small wooden object, the other held a carboard sign with ANYTHING HELPS scratched in crayon.

She quickly rolled down her window and held out a handful of bills. She accepted the wooden object he offered her in return and smiled back in response to his "Bless you, ma'am."

She tossed the object into the glovebox and fell in behind a car signaling for a left turn onto the westbound entrance ramp. A delivery truck descended the exit ramp toward its stop sign on her right. The car in front of her turned left and she began to follow.

The deafening crunch of metal on metal pushed her car hard to the left. The concrete pillar came fast. She blacked out.

* * * * *

Lucie awoke from her darkness with the steering wheel pressing into her chest. She struggled to breathe. Her passenger side door was gone and its seat was pushed into the dashboard. Reflections of red and blue lights bounced around her. She heard a woman's voice but couldn't understand her. She hurt everywhere.

Lucie couldn't see the tow truck that had pulled her car away from the pillar, the ambulance and the firetruck, and the two Corner Brook EMT's standing nearby. She couldn't see the fireman with a large pair of scissor-like jaws shear her door hinges, her steering column, the center pillar, and the legs of her seat, too. She couldn't see the man in tattered clothes watch it all helplessly, praying the pretty and generous young woman would be saved. All she could see was the mashed-up front end of the delivery truck that had run its stop sign.

As the fireman lowered the steering wheel away from her chest, she gasped for her first full breath of air. She felt herself being held against her seat while it slid back, tilted, turned, and rose up and out of the car.

The flashing lights blinded her as an EMT began treating her most obvious wounds. The EMT felt Lucie's arms, legs, and hips for broken or dislocated bones while asking her questions. What's your name? Where do you live? Can you move? Where does it hurt? Lucie couldn't answer any of them.

The EMT put a stethoscope to the side of Lucie's neck and listened. Then she and another EMT lifted Lucie out of her seat and placed her on a wheeled stretcher.

In her daze, Lucie watched the man in the tattered clothes shuffle his cart past the pillar, stop at the ditch beside the entrance ramp, and walk down into it. She felt herself being lifted into the ambulance as he loaded a coat, a backpack, and a damaged cardboard box into his cart and continued on his way.

12

Special investigations reporter Emma Walsh strode into the *News-Advertiser* at noon, climbed the stairs to the second floor, and hung her coat on the hook beside her desk. Today's edition of the *N-A*, as the *News-Advertiser* was called by its staff, lay on her chair, the result of a company policy that had given every issue to every employee for as long as the company had existed.

She'd had a difficult morning tracking down a source, and what she wanted before she began anything else was a hot cup of black coffee. She went to the breakroom, loaded the empty Cuisinart to make a fresh brew, and walked back toward her desk. On her way, she stopped at a colleague's cubicle to tell him that she'd run down that source: he'd confirmed the information they needed, and they could begin putting their piece together.

Like the other reporters' spaces on her floor, Emma's was a head-high cubicle of light blue fabric. It was large enough for an ample computer desk in its corner, a set of three matching shelves where she kept works-in-progress, two matching four-drawer filing cabinets, a comfortably padded ergo-chair on wheels, and a barrel-backed side chair for visitors.

Emma liked the *N-A*. It took good care of its staff, and its editors were thoughtful. She felt appreciated. In her view, that was unusual for a reporter who'd been with a company for only a few months. At her first and previous job, reporters were treated as if their only value was to keep the advertisers coming. She'd left that job after only four months for that reason.

She was about to return to the Cuisinart when her editor dropped last evening's edition of the *St. John's Telegraph* onto her desk and pointed to a story on the lower half of the front page. Emma picked it up, relaxed back into her chair, and read.

RALLIERS SUPPORT COYOTE BILL
Telegraph staff

A rally in support of a predator-hunting bill drew hundreds to the Colonial Building of St. John's yesterday, according to a statement released by the office of MHA Hunter Sullivan. "It was wonderful to see so many people from all walks of life come out from all over the province to show their support for my bill," Sullivan said.

"Within those sacred halls, a disparate and rag-tag group of negotiators came together in 1946," the statement continued, "and began to carve out for Newfoundland the most significant act in all its history—independence from Great Britain and a new partnership with Canada. And so it is with my bill. We shall declare our independence from the scourge of the mangy coyote and all his fearsome relatives, and create a new beginning for all of Newfoundland."

If passed, Sullivan's bill would open a year-round hunting season on the coyote and wolf and provide a bounty of $300 for each wolf and $175 for each

> coyote, far exceeding both the current bounty and the market value for pelts. Supported by hunters and outfitters but spurned by conservationists, the bill had advanced to second reading before being postponed by an emergency funding bill near the end of the provincial Assembly's spring/summer session.
>
> Representatives of the Department of Fish and Wildlife have expressed strong reservations about the bill, claiming it will divert badly needed funding away from valuable wildlife management activities. And conservationists recently clashed openly with outdoorsmen over the proposal near Awachanjeesh Pond in the south central part of the Island, as reported by the *News-Advertiser*.

Emma smiled, pleased that the *Telegraph* had picked up on her reporting.

> "The good people of The Rock deserve freedom from devastation and fear," Sullivan's statement continued. "I will therefore re-table my bill early during the fall session. With such broad support, I am certain it will pass very quickly. These loathsome creatures deserve the worst we can give them, and I will stop at nothing to assure they get it."

Wow, that man sure has a penchant for drama. She thought the *Telegraph* had covered the story well, but she considered whether her editor would want the *N-A* to print a companion article. As she saw it, Sullivan's bill, his rally, and the demonstration at Awachanjeesh were only remotely related to what now interested her most—to be the first to break the story of how the two men had died. She made a mental note to take it up with her editor if she found the time and tossed the *Telegraph* onto her side chair.

As she stood to get that long-awaited cup of coffee, a receptionist rapped on the edge of her cubicle wall and handed her a note. Emma thanked him and took the note and her cup to the Cuisinart, reading as she went. It said only "Barrett" followed by a phone number. She stopped and thought for a moment. *Barrett . . . Barrett . . . oh, right, the RCMP Barrett*. The Barrett she'd called after the old woman had told her about the dog and the man's arm. The Barrett she'd tried to reach early this morning before hunting down that source today.

She poured herself a cup, returned to her desk, and dialed. A voice answered on the fourth ring.

"You've reached the Grand Falls-Windsor office of the Royal Canadian Mounted Police," the voice began. "Vous avez atteint le Bureau de Grand Falls-Windsor de la Gendarmerie Royale du Canada. All lines are busy at the moment, your call will be answered by the first available receptionist. Toutes les lignes sont occupées en ce moment—" then came a click followed by the voice of a real person.

"Constable Barrett, may I help you? Gendarme Barrett, puis-je vous aider?" he asked.

"Constable Barrett, this is Emma Walsh, special investigations reporter for the News-Advertiser. You tried to return my call today about a man found dead beside Little River several days ago. What can you tell me?"

"Yes, Miss Walsh, I remember. That incident's under investigation at this time. I'm afraid there's not much I can tell you right now."

"No problem, I just have a few questions." She knew how this worked.

"As I said—"

"I sent you a photograph," she interrupted. "Did you recognize the device in it?

"Yes, I can tell you I've seen such a device before."

"Can you tell me what it is?"

"It's called a coyote getter. Used by sheep and cattle ranchers, mostly."

"Thank you, that confirms what I was told by a Fish and Wildlife officer.

"Fish and wildlife is involved in this?"

"Yes. Is that what killed the man you found beside Little River?"

"I can't reveal that information yet."

"But you know how he died, right?"

"I can't reveal that information at this time."

"So that's a *yes* to both of those questions, correct?"

Constable Barrett went silent, then huffed. "Miss Walsh, it seems you already know the answers to your questions." He paused. "And you heard none of them from me." He abruptly hung up.

She put her handset back into its cradle and smiled. She walked the narrow hallway between cubicles to a private office in the corner and knocked on its open door. Her editor looked up.

Emma told her the whole story, from the conversation she'd just had, to the call she'd received from the woman who lived beside Little River, to what Chief Joe had said about his Elder's death, their discovery of the entrails and the strange device near Medonnegonix Lake that Mitchell Gregg had told them was used to kill coyotes, and finished with the frightening incident she and Chief Joe had endured there. Then she described her idea.

Her editor called it a long shot, too circumstantial. She reminded Emma that she was supposed to be working on an important story that she'd expected to see in draft form hours ago. "Timing is everything, Emma" she said. "We can't hold it any longer."

Emma described how much trouble she'd had getting the source to talk, and only this morning had she been able to get what she needed. "First thing tomorrow morning, Todd or I will bring it to you," she promised.

Her editor threw up her hands but agreed. Emma returned to her desk and centered the rough draft of the overdue story on her desk as a reminder to tell Todd what she'd promised their editor. Then she dialed Chief Joe.

* * * * *

I had just finished a call when the telephone rang again. "Chief Joe?" I heard.

"Hello, Emma."

"Remember the photos I took when we were in the mountains?"

"Yes, of course. Mitchell and I spoke about them yesterday. He told me what that thing was."

"Right, he told me, too. I just finished taking to the RCMP about it. They're investigating how the man with a missing forearm died beside Little River. He said knew what the device in my photograph was, and that it may have killed him."

I sat abruptly upright. "He told you this?"

"Well, not in the way you might be thinking. We and the police have a special code for when they tell us something they don't want to tell us."

"Okay, I need to see this for myself. I'll call Mitchell, I think he should be there, too. Can you be ready by eight tomorrow morning?"

"Yep, and I'll bring the instructions from the son of the old woman."

"Good. I'll ask Mitchell to pick you up and meet me at *Jipuji'j* at ten."

"Got it. Tomorrow morning at ten o'clock."

13

It was about nine forty-five when I turned the Kawasaki onto the Bay d'Espoir Highway on my way to Jipu'ji'j. A large, black Ford pickup suddenly appeared in my mirrors. The winch, black grill guard, and off-road tires made it look bigger than it probably was and it was too close for my comfort. I moved to the right and slowed to let it pass, but it slowed with me. I sped up and it accelerated with me. I slowed again and it slowed, too. I turned the left side mirror to focus on the windshield. It was hard to see through the glare, but it looked like two people in the front seat, the driver ferociously waving me over as if he now wanted to pass after all. I pulled off into the dirt beside a Coast of Bays road sign and stopped, giving the driver an obvious opportunity to move on. But the truck stopped behind me.

Now I was worried. I put the Kawasaki in park, dismounted, and faced the truck directly, standing my tallest in hopes my posture would fend off a fight. The driver side door opened, and that was when I saw the emblem. NEWFOUNDLAND AND LABRADOR FISH AND WILDLIFE ENFORCEMENT OFFICER.

Mitchell Gregg stepped out and I saw Emma Walsh waive from the front seat.

"You gave me a scare, Mitchell," I said as I approached him, smiling. "Did they teach you how to do that in government driving school?"

"Heh, sorry about that," he said. We shook hands, then he thumbed over his shoulder at the truck. "New department rig. Saw it was you so decided to hang behind." He glanced at the Kawasaki as a half-smile took his face. "Besides, didn't want to blow past a rig like that, eh?"

I laughed. "And I thank you for that, Mitchell. I'll put it in high gear while you follow me the rest of the way to Jipu'ji'j. I promise a blistering pace."

"Got it. Be right behind you."

At Jupu'ji'j, I parked beside just outside the entrance gate. As I walked toward the truck, Emma stepped out with the ever-present camera slung around her neck. She greeted me with a bright smile and a cheerful "Morning!" I returned both the smile and the greeting.

"Nice day for a drive in the woods," she added.

I turned to scan the eastern horizon under a clear morning sky. The sun beamed at us from over the hills, and the air was so fresh it seemed to crackle. "I can hardly imagine a better one," I replied.

I reached to open the back door for myself but she stopped me. "You take the front seat." She glanced over at the Kawasaki then back at me with a knowing smile. "And I'll sit on a rear seat that that does not require me to hang on for my dear life."

Another laugh, then I climbed into the front seat while she took the rear.

We'd traveled several kilometers down the road when I noticed that Mitchell was uncharacteristically quiet. "Something on your mind, Mitchell?"

He glanced at me then looked back to the front. “Oh, prob’ly nothing but . . . well, you remember Lucie Headley, our intern, right?”

“From the helicopter. I do.”

“Reliable, always early,” he continued. “Loves her work, gladly works a Saturday if she thinks she needs to, that kind of thing.

“Left me a note said she was taking Wednesday off, then delivering those samples she collected the other day to a lab in Corner Brook Thursday morning. Left a message Wednesday she was on her way to Corner Brook already, said she’d be back last night. But no sign of her this mornin’.” He sighed. “But she’s young, you know? Maybe got caught up in things, new place and all, stayed an extra night. I worry just the same. Didn’t answer calls.”

“Ahhh, yes Mitchell, I knew something was up for you from very early today,” Emma offered from behind. “My guess is you have no daughter of your own.”

He shook his head. “Never married.”

“I thought so. I suspect Lucie has become the daughter you don’t have, and you worry a bit too much about her. She is, as you say, new to the province, and she’s a farm girl, too. She has a lot of new places to see and explore here.

“Not so long ago, I did the same thing, and often disguised my late arrival. It was a good thing that my employer didn’t keep close eyes on me, as I can see you do for her. Otherwise I wouldn’t be here with you today.” She paused briefly, then added “You’re a good man to be her first boss.”

“I think Emma has a point,” I chimed in.

Mitchell glanced briefly at Emma in his rear view mirror. “Yeah, maybe you’re right. Give her a little more time. She earns it, you know? Probably be there when I get back."

His spirits seemed to lighten after that and we picked up a little speed. Emma guided Mitchell according to the directions she'd been given by the old woman's son on the phone. Our goal was to find where Armless Man had been found, and maybe find clues about his death that will reveal how our Elder died.

We made our way up the same gravel road that Emma and I had travelled just two days ago, and took the road's left fork again to the same power line right-of-way. Mitchell stopped and dropped into four-wheel drive, then continued on the right-of-way to the Little River bridge crossing. There he stopped.

"Straight ahead, Emma?" he asked.

"No, Mitchell," she said looking at her notes. "From here he said we must go north through a long clearing—his one to our left, I believe — then follow a small creek to some marsh ponds. Go east below the marsh ponds to another large clearing, then north again. At the end of the second clearing, we should find what we are looking for. It is about two kilometers from this bridge, he said."

I turned in surprise to look back at Emma. "We were so close two days ago," I remarked.

"Okay, hang onto your hats," Mitchell said. "Gonna get rough."

The truck bounced and groaned, moving us over mounds and depressions at what seemed like only a few kilometers per hour. At its north end, Mitchell found a break in the trees and turned directly into the creek. Water rose to the middle of the hubcaps.

The trees opened up at the creek's mouth but Mitchel hugged them until we were well below the marsh ponds. There he followed another line of trees and a long mound covered in caribou moss to the second clearing, then worked us between a pair of smaller ponds to its far north end, where we saw the yellow tape.

"Looks like this is it," I said.

We stood looking at a part of the clearing marked out much like what Emma and I had found two days ago. Yellow tape with 'Police Line Do Not Cross' stamped on it encircled an area about thirty meters across. Outside of the circle there were signs of trucks and ATVs having parked there. Within it, numbered stakes were set in what seemed like random places, and the ground cover was trampled with the foot paths of what I assumed had been constables looking for whatever clues might have been hidden within it. Emma immediately began snapping photos while Mitchell walked a slow circle outside of the tape's boundary.

I presumed RCMP had taken photos here, too, then returned the body to the morgue to hopefully be identified by a family member or a friend. It was what I had expected to find, but at the same time it was a sad reminder of how much reverence for life was lost here. Armless Man had died not long ago, but only stakes and tape gave any hint that anything out of the ordinary had happened. No hint of the loss his death had left behind, not even a hastily made cross pounded into the ground. No sign of respect for the spirit that might return again and again for the lost arm, wanting to make itself whole again before departing this world forever.

Would Emma or Mitchell understand if I told them that the dead man's spirit might be here among us even now? I wasn't sure they would, and I chose to say nothing. We had come to hunt clues to Armless Man's death; the best thing to do was to focus on that goal. But I felt a presence here that I could explain only with the spiritual beliefs of my people.

"Mitchell, Emma," I called out. "We should comb the circle, inside and out. See what we find."

We lined up side by side with about a meter between us, Emma on the outside, me on the inside, Mitchell in the middle. We walked slowly around the taped circle together, eyes fixed on the ground around us, sweeping the grass and ground cover with our feet as we went. We'd gone about half way around when Emma stopped and pinched her nose.

"There's that smell again, Chief Joe," she said. What did you call them?"

"Entrails," I responded.

"Over there." She pointed to her right, near the trees at the edge of the clearing. We walked over to it.

She was right. The carcass of an animal lay in the grass. Its fur had been completely removed except around its legs and head. Mitchell brushed the grass aside with his foot, then squatted and held his hand over it. "A wolf, an' still warm," he said. "Man's the wolf's only predator. Warm carcass means the hunter or trapper might still be close by. An' this one's takin' 'em out of season."

I intently scanned our surroundings. Emma took photos.

I pointed to my right. "Mitchell, you take the trees that way. I'll take them this way. If he's here, we'll find him."

We headed off in our separate directions, he to the north, me to the south. I'd gone no more than twenty meters when something caught my attention. "Mitchell! Emma! Over here!"

"Find something, Chief?" Mitchell asked when they arrived. I pointed at my feet and they both squatted beside me.

"Well, I'll be damned," Mitchell said. "Another coyote getter. I see one of these things every couple of months, maybe less. Only legal in Alberta and Saskatchewan, but now ... now I'm beginnin' to think they're creepin' into this province faster than we know." Emma photographed it.

"Exactly the same getter Emma and I found where our Elder died shows up here. There has to be a connection," I asserted.

"Maybe," Mitchell admitted. "They're nasty, an' they'll make a man feel like he's gonna die. But nothing in my book says these things'll actually kill a man. Coyote, wolf, sure. But not a man."

"But the coincidence is just too strong to write off," I argued. "Couldn't there be something different about these getters? Like, I don't know, more poison in them than usual?"

"Can't see why anyone'd bother to do that," Mitchell answered. "It doesn't take much cyanide to kill 'em anyway. Besides, we're in the middle of nowhere here, no ranches for a dozen kilometers in any direction. Makes me question the brains of anybody who'd bother to put 'em here at all.

"And what makes you think this is what killed him?" he continued. "This one and the one you and Emma found before, they're both still live. They gotta go off in order to kill somethin'.

"And then there's that wolf over there," he went on. "Seems it would have been attracted to the getter if it's worth the parts it's made of. But here the thing sits, still live, like nothin's bothered it in weeks. All due respect, Chief, I think you're chasin' a goose."

He had me stumped. All I could do was stare blankly in return, like a dazed pup. *Am I jumping to conclusions again? Are Mitchell and Clarence Paul both right about me?* I began to doubt my instincts, and I wondered what my father would have thought at a time like this. Then Emma spoke up.

"Maybe you're right. But I now know Constable Barrett has been here, too. He knew what a getter was when I showed him a photo. And he told me off the record that RCMP thinks the getter is what killed him. So I think there's more here than we know."

Mitchell sighed. "Okay, back away for a minute, you two."

Emma and I stood and moved aside. With his face out of its line of fire, he slowly worked the stake loose and pulled it up, just as I had done two days ago. Emma took more photos, then we followed him as he carried it to the truck. He removed a small, lidded can from the center console, padded the getter gently with bubble wrap from the can, and sealed it inside. He strapped the can inside a small-animal carrier that had been firmly anchored in the bed of the truck.

"Evidence can will hold it till we get back," he said.

Then something cracked in the air and clanked into the side of its bed, right behind Emma. She turned her head to see what it was just as the boom of a high-powered rifle shook the air.

"EMMA, MITCHELL! DOWN!" I screamed. We dropped immediately. Emma covered her head with her hands. "Didn't we just do this?" she cried out.

I could see Mitchell on the ground on the other side of the truck. He had a *what-the-hell?* look in his eyes.

Then came a second crack and clank, this time into the door directly above me, followed by a second boom. I looked for an escape route, but the yards of open field around us would have made us easy targets long before we could get to cover. "Under the truck!" I called out, the only thing I could think of to do.

We clawed and twisted our way under and waited anxiously, expecting more. I looked at Emma, not believing what was happening. The fear on her face said the same thing. *How could we be under fire here, too? Were we followed? It surely couldn't be coincidence ... could it? And how long will we be pinned down this time?*

But a third shot never came. We waited longer. Still nothing.

We relaxed and were about to crawl out from under the truck when the sound of an ATV screamed at us from somewhere in the trees. It ricocheted from tree to tree, seeming to come from one direction, then another, then yet another.

"That has to be him!" I yelled. We scrambled out from under the truck and scanned the edge of the clearing for some sign of movement. "Damn it, where is he?" Mitchell called out.

The ATV burst into the meadow thirty meters to our south. It was moving fast toward the marsh ponds.

"There!" I yelled.

Mitchell had already started the engine when Emma and I jumped in. He jammed it into drive and hit the gas hard as he spun a U-turn and slammed his door closed. I grabbed the hand hold above my door to keep from falling out, and barely got it closed before we bounced and jolted across the meadow. My left hand groped for the dash while my right hand snapped my seatbelt into place. Emma cursed from the back seat as she clicked hers. Somehow, Mitchell had already managed to buckle his own.

Mitchell took us straight for the marsh ponds, hoping to head off the ATV. It was more agile than we were, and it artfully dodged the ruts and knobs and rocks that we couldn't. But Mitchell found a swale between the mounds and we began to gain on him. By the time he reached the marsh ponds, Mitchell had closed his lead to a few tens of meters. The swale veered to the left, putting us on a direct path to cut him off before he reached the creek. Mitchell continued to close the distance between us until only a few meters remained.

That was when the driver made a sharp left, crashed through the brush, and drove directly into the trees again. Mitchell swerved to follow, then slammed on the brake just as the brush clawed at his headlights. I jammed my hands onto the dash, bracing against the sliding halt. "Damn!" he uttered as I rebounded into the back of my seat.

I jumped out of the truck and ran after the ATV on foot. Emma and Mitchell followed right behind. We chased it down a hidden trail just wide enough for the ATV, ducking branches all the way to the creek. And there we stopped.

In front of us, at a shallow bend in the creek, lay a narrow bridge of loosely piled stones just under the surface. The track of an ATV had been scoured into them. Mitchell stood there with his hands on his hips and huffed out a sigh as the whine of the ATV died out somewhere on the other side.

"Damn," I said. "That was our chance to find out what's really going on."

* * * * *

Nineteen-year-old Billy McCabe had just finished a long morning of work. He wore his camouflaged uniform while he sat on his camouflaged Honda FourTrax at the edge of the Little River. He reached behind him into a small cooler on the ATV's rack and dug out a bottle of Crush cream soda and a plastic container of leftovers from the dinner his mom had made for him last night. He chewed his first spoonful as he watched and listened to the waves gently lap the shoreline, then washed it down with a sip of the soda.

Billy liked to do a good job at whatever he did. He especially liked this job because it took him to quiet, peaceful places like this one. He liked being where he could be away from people, especially ones who stared at him. What had happened hadn't been his fault, but sometimes he wanted to hide where no one could see the scar running from mid-forehead to ear.

He'd finished his lunch and returned the empty container and soda bottle to the cooler when he heard what sounded like a truck door slam somewhere behind him. He was about to ignore it when it happened twice more, and now he was curious about it. He pulled a rangefinder from the Honda's front pack and peered through it, trying to find a gap in the trees large enough to see into the meadow. He saw a large black pickup truck but the image wasn't very clear so he set the rangefinder aside.

From the scabbard buckled to the Honda's rear pack frame he removed a bolt-action rifle, the same one he'd used to win the local shooting competition three times in a row. He was proud of his ribbons, and he especially liked it when people cheered for him.

He raised the gun to his shoulder and peered through its scope. He adjusted the focus and power rings until the image of the truck became clear. He could see that it was parked near the station he had just tended. He saw two men and a woman, and they seemed to be looking for something by the yellow tape.

Billy had seen the yellow tape himself today. He knew the police sometimes did that when there'd been a crime, and he had wondered if the tape had anything to do with the dead man he'd seen there earlier this week. The man had been about his age and had worn the same kind of camouflage that Billy wore today. Billy had wanted to help him, but the man was already dead so Billy just took the used device he'd found and left. Billy had wanted to tell the police about the dead man later, but Mr. S had told him it was very important to keep everything about his job a secret.

Mr. S had also scolded him that day because he'd come back with one more used device than the number of new devices he'd started with. Mr. S was especially mad because that was the second time it had happened. The first time was when Billy had found a dead Indian man. Billy had to explain that he'd run out of new devices before he'd found the used ones by either of those dead men and couldn't replace them until his next trip out. Billy remembered that both times he'd returned a few days later to put a new device there, the dead men were gone and yellow tape was there instead.

Billy couldn't always see the two men and the woman very well because sometimes they would disappear behind a tree or some branches, but he kept watching. He saw the two men walk off in different directions, then saw one of them squat down. He saw the other man and the woman walk over to him, then they squatted down, too. Then they all stood up and they were looking at something together. Billy refocused the scope and zoomed in on it a little bit more to see what it was. It was the new device he had just planted there. He pulled his face back from the scope and gasped.

Then he remembered something. He returned his eye to the scope and focused it on their faces. He recognized one of the men and the woman as the same ones he had seen through his scope near Medonnegonix Lake just a couple days ago, the same ones that got away with a new device there, too. He gasped again.

"They can't do that!" he said nearly out loud. Mr. S had told him that it was very important that the places he called stations always have a new device there. Billy was to check each device every couple days, replace them with a new one if they looked used, and bring back all the used ones. Mr. S had said the devices were in lots of places here and in the Bay du Nord Wilderness, too. There were so many of them that he'd even given Billy a map with dots on it for all the stations. Mr. S had said it was a very important job.

So now Billy had no choice, he had to do something about the two men and the woman before they took away another device. Billy worried Mr. S would be very upset if he found out, because he'd already gotten into trouble about the two dead men. But Billy knew he couldn't walk over there and tell them to leave it alone. That would give away the secret. Billy thought hard about what to do.

He thought about trying to scare them away like he did the last time. He remembered that they got away with the device then anyway. But he needed to get that device back and scaring them was the only thing he could think of.

He took a cartridge from a box in the pack next to the scabbard and loaded it into the rifle's chamber. He rested the barrel on the Honda's handlebar, pulled the rifle into his shoulder, and laid his cheek on the stock. He turned the focus ring slightly and adjusted the elevation to compensate for drop. He aimed the crosshairs between the trees at the side of the truck's bed just behind the woman. He took a deep breath, and exhaled to steady himself. Then he carefully squeezed the trigger.

The bullet hit the side of truck. *Perfect. Close enough to scare them but not hurt them.* Billy waited for them to drop the device and drive away, but they didn't so he reloaded. This time the bullet hit one of the doors just above a man's head.

But they still weren't leaving, and now Billy realized he had a problem—the box of cartridges was empty. He was certain they'd come looking for him, and then he'd be in even bigger trouble because the secret would be out. So Billy decided to do the only other thing he could think of—drive away as fast as he could.

He jumped on his FourTrax and twisted the throttle hard. At the meadow, the truck was already behind him. He dodged rocks and ruts but it was getting closer. He turned sharply into the brush and trees. His front wheels dug into the creek bed, and he almost flew over the handlebars. He recovered and put as much distance between him and the truck as he possibly could.

He was about to congratulate himself on his getaway when it suddenly struck him that he had another problem. He stopped behind a clump of trees where he couldn't be seen and began to worry once again.

Billy had always tried to do his very best at his job, but now that man and woman had taken another new device. Billy remembered feeling both sad and mad at the same time after Mr. S scolded him the first time when that happened. Even though he knew he had followed the rules, he worried that Mr. S would blame him anyway. He leaned against a rock and thought hard.

Then it came to him. He could tell Mr. S that he just didn't find any more used devices in the woods today. Billy liked that idea. Now, he would get to keep his own secret.

He felt much better now, and that was good because it was time to go. He had to meet Mr. S at their secret place by noon, get home in time to watch his favorite afternoon TV show, and take his medicine.

Before he left, he wanted to figure out how much extra money he'd earn today. Mr. S had told him to look for any dead coyotes or wolves while doing his job and that if he skinned them and brought back their pelts, he would get an extra five dollars for each one.

Billy had once asked Mr. S why they died. Mr. S had said that sometimes they just get sick and then they die. That made Billy sad. He didn't like it when animals got sick and died.

Today Billy had four pelts and they were all on the Honda's front rack. He calculated out loud. "F-five plus f-five is ten, plus f-five is f-fifteen, plus f-five is twenty. Twenty dollars!" He smiled because he could give it to his mom and she could use it to pay bills.

* * * * *

Back at the truck, a thought struck me. "But you know what? That bridge tells us something after all."

"An' what's that?" Mitchell asked.

"It says that the guy on the ATV has a reason to be here, that he's been here before and he'll come back again. The question is, who, when, and why. I can't tell you the when, but my hunch is that the who and why have something to do with that getter."

We examined the bullet holes. "Interesting," I said. "He could have hit the gas tank or a tire or one of us, but he didn't."

Mitchell pulled his finger away from the hole in the side of the door and sighed. "Well, good aim or bad, I'm gonna have a hell of a time explainin' this to the motor pool."

I was exhausted from this morning's events, but my mind swarmed as we climbed back into the truck. *Why did we find an unspent coyote getter here when RCMP didn't? What would the lab tell us about them? What was the connection in all this to the four eagles? Was everything just another curious piece of an unsolvable puzzle?*

On the way back, Emma scooted forward to the back of the front seat and began asking Mitchell questions. Where did the getters come from? Who made them? If they're illegal, how did they get into the Province? Who brought them in?

"Can't help you there," was all he said. She sat back and stared out the window in silence, as if her mind was working hard at something. But for me, this was the second time the tone of his voice told me he knew more. I began to wonder if I could still trust him.

Back at Jupu'ji'j, Mitchell and Emma waited while I warmed up the Kawasaki. They followed me along the Bay d'Espoir Highway back to the administration building. I told Mitchell I'd take both his evidence can and the getter in the old fox den to the one person I trusted to tell me what was in them. We waved goodbye as he and Emma drove away.

14

Emma Walsh returned to her office after her outing with Mitchell Gregg and Chief Joe, still on edge from being shot at for a second time this week. She wondered whether she should ask her editor for a different assignment, let someone else risk their life to find out whatever they needed to know about coyote getters and the two dead men. *No*, she decided, *this could be my first big story and I'll be damned if I'm gonna let anyone else get their hands on it.*

She turned to her computer to compose an article about their discovery this morning. The *Telegraph* with its article about Sullivan's rally still sitting on her side chair caught attention. Her eyes went to the very last line. "Good God" she said out loud. She re-read the entire article, then focused on the closing quote from Sullivan: "These loathsome creatures deserve the worst we can give them, and I will stop at nothing to assure they get it."

She knew the ramifications of her conclusion were serious. Her call to Sullivan's office yielded a no-comment, and the RCMP gave its usual ongoing-investigation response. She decided to gamble and strode to her editor's office.

Emma reviewed for her how the hunter and demonstrator clash had played out after Sullivan arrived, and that Sullivan had been adamant that coyotes and wolves must be eradicated. She reminded her that the *N-A* had received notice of the demonstration from two sources – one, the demonstrators, which would have been expected, and two, Sullivan. She mentioned again her conversation with Constable Barrett of the RCMP, then described the discoveries she, Mitchell Gregg, and Chief Joe had made at the sites where two men had already died, the too-strong coincidence of finding exactly the same coyote getter at each of those sites, and coming under fire both times they tried to retrieve the getters themselves. She said she suspected there were more getters out there and that someone must be watching them closely.

She added that Mitchell Gregg had said coyote getters were federally regulated and not legal for use in this Province. She reasoned that whoever was bringing them in must be influential enough to get them past the authorities and smart enough to not get caught, which also suggested that someone else may have been hired or bribed to do the dirty work of planting them in the wilderness. "It must be him," she ended. "He can be the only one with motive, character, reputation, and means to do such a terrible thing."

Her editor considered that. "And if you're wrong?"

"I'm not."

Confident, aren't you? Okay, let's go with it," she said at last. "No accusations, we don't want any legal trouble. But give enough to let the readers decide for themselves. Let's see what we flush out of the bushes."

Emma beamed inside as she stood "And be sure to thank Todd for finishing your other story," her editor added with a knowing glance.

Emma could feel her face flush. "Yes, ma'am." She quickly returned to her desk and typed out her story.

COYOTE DEVICE IMPLICATED IN DEATHS
Emma Walsh, News-Advertiser

Contact with unlicensed predacide devices is one of the causes under investigation in the recent deaths of two men in remote areas of south central Newfoundland, according to an RCMP officer who requested anonymity. The names of the men have been withheld pending the conclusion of the investigation.

More commonly known as M44s or coyote getters, these devices are intended to exterminate coyotes that wander onto sheep and cattle ranches.

While these devices are still uncommon in the province, their growing presence is troubling to wildlife officials. "These small, capsule-like devices are set close to the ground and are difficult to see," said Provincial Wildlife Enforcement Officer Mitchell Gregg. "Wrapped in a scented bait, they unleash toxic sodium cyanide powder when bitten by the predator, inflicting a rapid death. They are federally controlled and not approved for use in Newfoundland and Labrador. Beware of them. They do not discriminate between predators and other wildlife, they can be deadly to pets and children, and they can inflict serious injuries on adults. I urge anyone coming into contact with one to report its location and stay safely away."

Coyote and wolf populations have grown steadily since first arriving in the mid-1980s. But the relatively sudden presence of these devices in the most remote parts of this province is unexpected, for predators in those areas are no threat to livestock. Conservationists argue predators are critical to maintaining the natural balance among species, and they have long railed against the use of these devices as inhumane, ineffective, and counterproductive.

MHA Carson Sullivan has proposed sweeping legislation to eradicate coyotes and wolves. In a statement reported by the *Telegraph* yesterday, Sullivan described coyotes as "loathsome creatures" that deserve "the worst we can give them" and he assured his rally that he would "stop at nothing to be certain they get it."

Citing its ongoing investigation, the RCMP chose not to divulge who brings these devices into the province, how they arrive, or how they come to be planted in the wilderness.

15

When I'd called Anna earlier today, she'd said she'd love to see me again and that our past year apart had been too long. And I looked forward to seeing her again, too. But an unexplained apprehension filled me as I drove into Corner Brook in the aging sedan I'd borrowed from the motor pool. *Had that year cooled her feelings despite her words? Had it cooled mine?* I'd been a stranger then, trying to learn what or who had killed my father and reacquainting myself with this land after nineteen years away. She was Dr. Annamarie Chartier, an established professor and an expert in her field. Now, I was Chief of the Mi'kmaq First Nation and she was a university department head. Our lives had changed.

She'd said she'd be working her usual late hours but I could meet her at the main entrance at six. That's also when I'd deliver to her the two coyote getters in the trunk.

I approached the two-story, earthen-brown brick building housing the School of Science and Environment with Mitchell's evidence can and the small cardboard box holding the other getter. I climbed the landing, passed between two brick pillars, and walked under the second-floor overhang to the double glass doors. I was just about to rap on one of them with my free hand when I saw her through the glass walking toward me. She pushed the door open and greeted me with a bright, green-eyed smile. A waft of outdoor air buffeted the ends of her open lab coat and blew a tuft of deep brown hair onto the side of her face. *Still stunningly beautiful.* My breath caught in my throat as she approached.

"Oh, Peter!" she said, standing on her toes and throwing her arms around my neck. "How wonderful it is to see you again!"

My apprehension suddenly vanished and the reflex to just hold her took over. The subtle scent of her hair took me back. We stood there in our embrace for what seemed like minutes.

We talked about old times as we passed through the atrium under flags of indigenous nations and nation states of the world and up a wide curved stairway. Inside her office, I set the box and evidence can on her desk. She began to open the box as I sat down in the guest chair. "And what do we have here?"

"Be careful, they're coyote getters. They could go off on you if you handle them wrong."

"Coyote getters?" She stopped and sat down in her chair. "Oui, I have heard of them from colleagues in the prairie provinces. For livestock protection. Nasty devices, these things. Why have you brought them here?"

"Mitchell and I found them in and near the Bay du Nord. I think getters like these might have killed a man, maybe two—one of them being one of our Elders. I hope you can tell us if there's anything unusual about them."

"You have lost an Elder? I am so sorry, Peter. That must be awful."

I sighed. "He was a good man, and truly an asset for me as I became chief. He is greatly missed by everyone."

There was a respectful pause before she began again.

"Forgive me for jumping back into business, but in what way might these coyote getters be unusual?"

"I'm not sure, really. Mitchell says they normally can't kill a man, that there isn't enough cyanide in them to do that. So if they did kill those men—like I think they did—they'd have to pack a lot more cyanide or maybe something else. He thinks I'm wrong, that those two men died from something completely different."

She seemed to think about that. "I see. Fortunately, we have developed a special procedure for cases in which we do not know what the analyte is. How soon will you want results?"

"As soon as you can get them."

"Very well. I can assign a technician to work on it this weekend. I would say two days will be adequate. Also, since you and Mitchell appear to be working together on this, I will contact him before we begin. It is quite possible that I may be able to bill our services to the standing contract we have with his department. I will contact you and Mitchell as soon as we have results, and Mitchell will receive a full written report shortly afterward."

"Perfect."

"All I need now is chain-of-custody."

"Chain of custody?"

"Yes, a form that tells who has handled the coyote getters to assure the results will hold up in court, should it go that way."

I nodded. "Okay, but here's the thing. I can sign for the one in the box. Mitchell collected the one in the can."

"Then I will begin with yours. Should I need Mitchell's, we shall have to work out an arrangement after the fact. It is not the best of circumstances, but I have seen it survive cross-examination before."

She removed a form from a file drawer in her desk and passed it to me. I filled in the blanks and signed it. Then she signed it, too.

"Excellent, Peter." She laid the form on her desk and stood.

I stood, too, not knowing what to do next. "Thanks, Anna," I said at last. "I guess I'll be going, then.

"Wait, Peter. Allow me to accompany you. It is time that I call my day to an end, and it would be especially nice to walk with you." She draped her coat over her arm and grabbed her briefcase. I held the doors for her as we walked to the entry.

Outside, the parking lot was now nearly empty. We walked together and stopped beside a blue Mazda Miata. The forgotten image of caribou in the headlights flashed in my mind.

"No red MGB," I joked.

She sighed and smiled. "Yes, one year ago. We sent it to its grave, didn't we."

"So we did."

She stood on her toes and reached up to kiss me. It was warmer than I expected or thought I deserved. Our smiles lingered as we said goodnight. She turned to her car. My heart shouted *Say something! Do something!* but I froze. A sad emptiness grew inside me again as I watched her drive away.

16

At seven forty-five the next morning, Dr. Annamarie Chartier disembarked Corner Brook Transit's Route 1 bus across from the roundabout by the Pittman Wing Residences. She took the sidewalk along University Drive to the Backlot, the student union building for Sir Wilfred Grenfell College. She pulled open one of its double glass doors, and made her way to the coffee bar.

This was her favorite time of the day because the Backlot wasn't yet swamped with students and faculty rushing for coffee or an eat-on-the-run breakfast before an early class. She recently had come to enjoy a casual early morning visit with the new student barista behind the counter. This morning, they were talking about nothing in particular when the student became more serious. She said her history major was unsatisfying and she was thinking about changing.

"To what?" Dr. Chartier asked. "What do you love?"

The student let her eyes drift downward.

"Well, that's the hard part, professor," she answered. "I thought about Poli Sci, but that means transferring and it doesn't seem right anyway. My friends and I, we're really worried about climate change. Everything around us depends on what happens. But we feel helpless, you know?

I'd give anything to make a difference there. I just don't know where to begin," the student ended.

"It seems you have a passion for the Earth," Dr. Chartier offered after a thoughtful pause.

"You know, I think I do," the student responded.

"Might you consider environmental science? The field could suit you well and prepare you a meaningful future, too. If you wish, you may come to my office this week. I will be happy to tell you about it." She handed the student a calling card from her briefcase. "Perhaps it is a good fit for you."

The barista passed a grande decaf mocha over the counter. Dr. Chartier took a sip, then offered a smile.

The barista studied the card and nodded. "Yeah, I think I might like that. Thank you, Professor Chartier."

Annamarie Chartier picked up her briefcase, said "au revoir" to the barista, and walked to the doors at the far end of the Backlot. She pushed at the crash bar with her hip and climbed a flight of stairs to the second floor of the Environmental Studies Wing of Grenfell's Arts and Sciences building. There she strode down a long hallway lined with photographs of former students who had become important faculty or environmental innovators in business and government. She passed two of its seven classrooms and one of its three state of the art laboratories before she entered the office with this sign beside its door:

DEPARTMENT OF ENVIRONMENTAL STUDIES
OFFICE OF THE CHAIR
ANNAMARIE CHARTIER, PHD

Her assistant, Claire, was already at her desk when Dr. Chartier passed by with a friendly greeting.

She was scanning her email when she heard a male voice in the outer office speaking to Claire but asking for her. Claire asked if he had an appointment. As the man became insistent, Dr. Chartier rose from her chair and stopped him just outside her door.

"Bonjour, monsieur, I am Annamarie Chartier. How is it that I may help?" she asked. The man stopped.

His face was dark and leathery, as if aged by the wind and sun. His hair appeared not to have been washed or combed for days and, except for a new-looking coat, his clothes were frayed and worn. He stood with a premature hunch at his shoulders, and a backpack hung so loosely there it seemed ready to fall off.

He pointed to a damaged box under his arm. "For you," he said in a gravelly voice. "Your name on top, same as by the door." He offered it to her.

She took the box in both hands and looked at it with a scientist's curiosity. Three of its corners were crumpled and it had a long gash across one side. And he was right: it was addressed to her at the School of Science and Environment. She placed the box on her desk, sliced the packing tape with a scissor blade, and spread open the flaps.

The first thing she found inside was a purchase order from Mitchell Gregg's department. She looked up in astonishment.

"Merci, monsieur, but . . . how did you get this?" she asked. "And how did you find me here?"

He lowered his gaze and wiped what she thought was a tear from the corner of his eye. "Wednesday . . . young woman . . . accident," he said at last. He looked up at Dr. Chartier again. "Hurt pretty bad . . . ambulance took her. I found the box by the road."

"She had a pretty smile," he continued. "She helped me with money just before the accident. I rode a bus today as far as I could . . . then I walked."

He shrugged the backpack off his shoulders and caught a shoulder strap with his right hand. He gave it to Dr. Chartier. "And this," he added. "It was hers, too.

"And this, too, but—" His eyes pleaded for sympathy as his hands went for the coat's storm flap. "—it's so cold now."

Dr. Chartier suddenly understood. "Monsieur, please have a seat." She pointed to the chairs against the wall opposite Claire's desk. "And would you like a cup of coffee and something to eat?"

"I . . . I don't want to be trouble, ma'am."

"Not at all," she answered. She looked toward her assistant. "Claire?"

Claire smiled and rose, then walked down the hall. The man sat.

"Monsieur, may I have your name?" Dr. Chartier asked.

"Zach. Zach Thomas."

She offered her hand. "It is my pleasure to meet you, Zach Thomas."

He accepted her handshake. "Likewise, ma'am."

"And from where did you come today?" she asked.

"Steady Brook, ma'am."

"Do you live there?"

He sighed heavily. "Sometimes. Depends."

"I see. Will you excuse me for just one moment, please?" she asked. He nodded as she stood and started toward her office. She closed the door part way, sat at her desk, and dialed.

Claire returned a few moments later with coffee, a croissant, and an éclair from a pastry box left in the breakroom by a faculty member. Zach set the coffee on the floor beside him and took the napkin-wrapped pastries in his hands.

He eagerly began with the éclair. "Thank you so much, ma'am," he said between bites. He was halfway through it when he noticed Claire staring. He stopped.

"Oh, sorry, ma'am. I . . . I haven't eaten since yesterday morning."

"You go right ahead, sir. You have no need to apologize and there are more where those came from. Just say the word."

A few minutes later, Dr. Chartier returned and sat beside him.

"Zach Thomas, I have what I hope is welcome news for you. The Salvation Army Citadel here in Corner Brook will have a vacancy for you tonight, and a meal too, and for several weeks more if you wish to stay. Our university is often in need of good laborers, and we have come to prefer graduates of the Citadel's fine work training program. Does this interest you?"

"Uh . . . I don't have . . . I mean . . . " he stammered.

"No need for worry, I am happy to do this. It is my appreciation for what you have done for me today. You need only say yes, if that is what you wish."

She noticed him staring blankly at his wringing hands. She tried to imagine his dilemma: *A rigged-up shelter somewhere, begging for whatever anyone might give him. Or fresh meals, get paid, sleep in a warm bed.*

"Yes, Ma'am, I'd like that," he said at last.

She broke into a broad smile. "Very well, then. But I must confess I had counted on your affirmative response. Someone will come momentarily to help you collect your things, then take you to the Citadel. It is only a short distance, and you may wait here until then."

He balanced his coffee and croissant on the chair between his knees, took her hand in both of his, and looked her directly in the eye. "I will repay your kindness, ma'am, I promise."

She put her other hand on his and returned his look. "And I have no doubt you will." She retrieved her hands and sat back. "Now then, if you will excuse me again, I have a small business matter I must take care of." She stood and returned to her office.

Zach finished his coffee and croissant. When Claire offered him an orange juice, he nodded with a smile and a "Yes please, ma'am." She went to the breakroom, returning just as Dr. Chartier reentered the front office.

A few moments later, a young man stepped into the doorway and rapped on the jamb. They turned their heads.

"Hi. Ken from the Citadel. I have orders to pick up a Mr.—" he checked the note in his hand, "—Zach Thomas."

"Bonjour, Ken. This is your man."

Dr. Chartier turned to Zach. "Well, Zach Thomas, it seems it is time for you to go." She gave a smile and shook his hand as they stood up together. "Thank you again for your kindness. I wish you very much luck, and I hope I may see you again."

He turned back and smiled as he left.

She then turned her attention to the box still on Claire's desk. She folded back the flaps again and removed the rest of the paperwork sitting on top of its contents. She found a request for analysis and a chain-of-custody form, both bearing the Fish and Wildlife Department's name and logo. She set them aside.

She lifted out a container shrouded in insulating wrap. She peeled back the wrap and lifted out the container. "Oh my, Claire. Look at this!"

The container was icy cold. She examined its sides and was pleased to see that whatever had damaged the box had not compromised the container. She replaced the insulating wrap and handed it to her assistant.

"Claire, this must go to the freezer immediately, please," she said. "And ask the lab to check the condition of its contents."

Claire carried it off while Dr. Chartier sat to examine the analytical request. *GC mass spec scan, animal tissue, organic toxin hazard anticipated*, it said. Then she turned her attention to the chain-of-custody. The printed name and signature of a Lucie Headley appeared consistently on both forms. She looked for the earliest signature, for that would determine how much time remained before the samples must be extracted and prepared for analysis. She learned that they'd been collected Monday. Today was Friday. She recalled the holding time for the requested analysis was seven days. That didn't allow much time, but it could still be done if she put a technician on overtime right away. Everything else seemed to be in order.

Curiosity caused her to open the backpack. Inside she found a day's change of clothes, a wallet, a cell phone, and a ticket stub for yesterday's morning tour of Western Brook Pond. She studied the driver license inside. The name on it matched the one on the chain-of-custody. An uneasiness grew inside her.

She awakened the cell phone, touched playback, and listened. The message confirmed her fears.

Three rings. Four rings. Her fingers drummed the desk anxiously as she waited. At the fifth ring, a male voice answered.

"Fish and Wildlife. How may I help you?" it said.

"Bonjour, monsieur," she responded quickly.

"Mitchell Gregg, please. Annamarie Chartier, Grenfell College."

"One moment. I'll connect you." Subscription music finished a Gordon Lightfoot song while she waited. Mitchell Gregg picked up just as it ended.

"H'lo, Annamarie! Long time. How've you been?"

"Bonjour, my friend. Please pardon my abruptness. I believe you have a Lucie Headley in your employ. Have you heard from her recently?"

He went silent. "I'm afraid to ask why you're asking," he said at last.

"Forgive me, Mitchell. I believe I have some bad news for you."

17

I'd taken a midmorning walk along the George Drew Trail to Muskrat Point, and I now sat there alone on the small, solitary bench beside the shore, looking across the glassy surface of the Conifer River's wide mouth, listening to its almost silent flow. The splash of an osprey's unlucky dive was its only disturbance.

This was one of my favorite escapes. I stretched out on the bench and closed my eyes. I pulled the collar of my jacket around my neck and allowed the subtle burble of ripples beyond my feet to become the healer whose only task today was to clear the fog and distractions from my mind. I heard the osprey's second splash, but I ignored the temptation to see if it fared better this time. Images of the Old Ones began to flow through my fading awareness. I settled into that private place between awake and asleep.

A boy is lost in the woods. He finds the wigwam of Muin'skw, the Bear Woman. Muin'skw has Power and appears as a human. She gives the boy berries and nuts from her winter stores, and soon he thinks he will stay with his new family forever. In spring, he helps Muin'skw and her cubs hunt mice and smelt. But Muin'skw tells the boy she hears voices and that he must climb a tree to see if hunters are coming. They are from his village and soon they surround the boy. They take the boy home, and he is happy to be among his people again.

I woke up and sat bolt upright and rubbed my eyes with the heels of my hands. *Of course! Mickey John was the one person who knew more than any of us!* I resolved to see him, but there was something I needed first. I rushed back along the trail and went straight to my office.

When I arrived, I found a man standing outside my door. He looked to be about my age, and lean with long, dark hair. He wore denim under an open trench coat. He was rocking from foot to foot as if impatient. He walked quickly toward me as I approached, offering his hand.

"Ross Nelson, Save The Predators," he said. He took the hand I extended in return and gave it a gentle grasp.

"Chief Joe," I responded. "I don't have much time right now, but you're welcome to come in for a few minutes." I unlocked my door and he followed me in. I directed him to the chair beside my desk as I sat in my own.

"What can I do for you, Mr. Nelson?"

"Quite a bit, I hope. Let me explain. Nefarious forces are at work around us, Chief, even as we speak." His hands began to animate his words. "People who scour minerals from the earth, leaving their ugly scars behind. People who take oil from the ground, leaving toxic ground water in their wake. People who ravage the forest, leaving barren and eroded hillsides. People who pollute our lakes and rivers with the wastes of manufacturing in the name of better living. In short, people who will never see the value of the world as it was given to us, people who take from it only for the sake of power and profit.

"What I'm here about today is the newest threat. I'm here to seek your support against Assemblyman Sullivan and his allies—those who want to destroy the natural cycle of birth and death that keeps our living world in balance.

These people want to exterminate every living predator on this island for the benefit of a handful of hunters, outfitters, and a few scattered ranchers. I'm appealing to you for support. We have to save the natural world from his cruel plot, a scheme that will surely eliminate critical species from the food chain and upset the natural way of things for centuries to come. It will be a monumental battle, but we can win it if we act now.

"And according to the news, he's already trying to kill them off himself. I'm sure you've seen it. Coyote getters, right in the forests where they live. And two people have already died from them. The man has a lot of gall. He's sick if you ask me." He paused again.

It felt like a speech designed for a captive audience. I didn't appreciate his manner or his lack of respect. I held my response.

"So what do you say? I hope you're ready to join the battle against the greed and audacity of this ignorant man and his allies. I'd like you by my side. We can wipe the stain of this outrageous endeavor from the face of the Earth."

That seemed to be the end of his pitch. I paused for a few moments to consider the implications of his request.

"I sympathize with your concern, Mr. Nelson," I began. "My ancestors learned long ago to respect the land that provides for us, something I wish all people on this planet would learn. And I've learned something about Assemblyman Sullivan myself recently. But I have both a council and a people that I must consult before I could put my nation behind this. We are at last making strides in regaining our traditional role in matters such as this very one where our ancestral lands are involved, and I do not want to jeopardize that progress. So while I appreciate your concern and your mission, on the whole it's unlikely your offer is something I could agree to at the moment."

He sat back in his chair and folded his arms. “With all due respect, Chief, I hope you reconsider. This is an opportunity to reshape how decisions affecting the natural world are made in this province.”

He waited for my response. I glanced at my watch. “I’m afraid I’m wasting your time, Mr. Nelson. And I have an appointment in a few minutes, so I hope you’ll excuse me while I prepare.”

He looked away and stared at the wall as if deciding what to say next. He turned to face me and put an elbow on my desk. “I see you don’t really understand how important this matter is, Chief. The natural process of evolution on this island will be altered forever if Sullivan has his way. Think of it—this could be your legacy! What an incredible example you’d be setting for your children, and their children after them!“

Now I was beginning to lose my patience. “With all due respect, Mr. Nelson, I’ll determine what I want my legacy to be and how I’ll achieve it.”

His face reddened and he stared straight ahead for long moments. Then he stood, leaned over and stiff-armed the top of my desk. His scowled and his voice deepened. “Your legacy will be that of a man afraid to confront the forces that control him!”

I rose to face him. “That will be all, Mr. Nelson,” I said calmly. “It’s time for you to go now.”

He glared angrily, then stormed to my door where he stopped and looked back. He thrust a pointed finger at me.

“You will soon regret that you refused me!” Then he turned and left.

I sat back down into my chair and ran my hands through my hair. For a moment, I wondered where people like him came from, but I decided I didn’t have time to worry about that right now. I wanted to reach Emma before my appointment. I dialed her office number, hoping she would be there. She answered on the first ring.

"Emma Walsh, *News-Advertiser.*"

"Hi, Emma, Chief Joe. Are you busy? I need a favor."

"Yeah, sure! What is it?"

"Remember the photos you took of that coyote getter we found this morning? I need a few, both when it was in the ground and after Mitchell pulled up the stake. Any chance you could send them to me right away?"

"You bet. Coming right your way."

"And by email, please. I need full size copies. And quickly."

"Can I ask what's up?"

"You may, and I promise to explain it to both you and Mitchell very soon."

After hanging up, I rose and walked to the window, stood with my arms folded across my chest, and looked out once again on the stillness of the mouth of the Conifer River. I had a lot on my mind—Leon and Mickey John, Armless Man, the identical getters we'd found where they died. The connection between them seemed so obvious, but at the same time so elusive. And my upcoming appointment, while completely unrelated, was troubling just the same. There had been a new challenge to our hunting and fishing rights. This would be our strategy meeting to decide how we would approach the upcoming hearing. I had only minutes left to prepare myself for what had always been a heated topic.

But the serenity of the Conifer had always brought a calmness into my heart and settled my mind. It was no different today. I took in its beauty for a few minutes more, sighed a relaxed sigh, then turned away from the window and began to make my way back toward my desk.

That was when I heard the crackle of glass and a loud, sharp report behind me. Without thinking, I turned around. In the center of my window, I saw a small hole surrounded by a coarse, white circle within a star of hairline cracks. I dropped to the floor and covered my head just as the second shot punctured the glass.

I waited, certain there were more to come. But none did. I rolled onto my back and saw two small bullet holes in my ceiling. I got to my hands and knees and crawled to the window. I peered out just above the sill, but I could see no one.

Then something black came flying toward me. I turned away quickly, ducked to the floor, and shielded my head again. The window exploded and shards of glass fell all around me. There were loud thumps on the floor at the other end of the room.

I opened my eyes and lifted my head. The sounds of a screaming engine and tires spewing gravel came at me through the broken window. I jumped up to see who had done this, but saw no one. I ran into the hallway. I hammered on Clarence Paul's door and shook the knob, but it was locked. I bolted down the stair to the other end of the building and out the door. I saw only a long trail of dust headed north toward Highway 365. "Damn!" I shouted.

I stood there in shock, shaking needles of glass from my clothes. The head of our administrative staff came running out with an equally shocked look on her face. She said she and her aides, Dave and Lisa, had gotten everyone under their desks when they'd heard the shots, but Dave had seen enough of the vehicle to get a description and was on a radio call with Clarence Paul now.

Relief swept over me. "I'm glad you're all safe, Millie," I said.

"As we are of you, Chief Joe," she answered. "And I'll reschedule today's meeting. I'd say this is no longer the best time for it."

Was she ever right about that. "Wela'lin. Let's try again in a week or two."

"Any idea who would do this?"

"Third time this week and not a clue," was all I said, but I was rapidly becoming weary of being somebody's target.

With that, she went back to her office and I to mine. I brushed the glass off my side chair and sat down. Was this Ross Nelson getting even for my refusing him? Was it whoever had shot at Emma, Mitchell, and me earlier? Or could this have been some kind of mistake? I stared again at the holes in the ceiling, as if they somehow held the answer. And then I remembered the thumps.

I found it on the floor in the corner of my office: a river rock, dark and heavy. A folded piece of paper was taped around it. I removed the paper, unfolded it, and read.

> Good Injuns stay out of what ain't their business.
> Be a good Injun . . . or be a dead one.

What business was I supposed to stay out of? And who wanted me dead if I didn't? The only answer that came was that I must be getting close to something big.

18

Ross Nelson had rented an efficiency apartment in the remodeled basement garage of a plain brown house in Gander. One tiny window looked out on a cluttered alley and cast only a dull glow onto the kitchen wall. It was too close to the airport's departure path for his liking, and like a poke in the eye it had a Sullivan Avenue address. The only good thing was the Tim Horton's just a block away. He'd complained to his coordinator, but all he'd gotten in return was a curt "Donations aren't what they used to be."

But there was good news today. Sitting on the only stool for his tiny breakfast bar, he took a long sip from a rewarmed cup of Tim's Original Blend and grinned from ear to ear. On the bar in front of him lay the *News-Advertiser* he'd picked up on his return from Milltown. He leaned forward and read for the second time the three paragraphs he'd already circled with a bright, yellow marker.

> Contact with unlicensed predacide devices is one of the causes still under investigation in the recent death of two men in remote areas of south central Newfoundland, according to an RCMP officer who requested anonymity. More commonly known as M44s or coyote getters, these devices are intended to deter coyotes from sheep and cattle ranches.

> MHA Hunter Sullivan has proposed sweeping legislation to eradicate these animals. In a statement released by his office yesterday, he described coyotes as "loathsome creatures" that deserve "the worst we can give them" and he assured his rally he would " . . . stop at nothing to be certain they get it."
>
> Citing its ongoing investigation, the RCMP chose not to divulge who brings these devices into the province, how they arrive, or how they come to be planted in the wilderness.

There they were, the very words he'd been looking for. Words that had all but said it out loud—Sullivan was the one responsible for the coyote getters that killed those two men and who knows how many coyotes and wolves. Now he had the ammunition he needed for his next demonstration. He was certain he could kill Sullivan's bill before the next sitting of the Assembly and Sullivan himself would go down in coyote-getter flames. Which meant he could soon be back in Halifax after having saved Newfoundland's coyotes and wolves in record time. He could already feel a national conservation award in his hands.

* * * * *

Minister Carson aka Hunter Sullivan sat alone on the Victorian settee in his second floor living room as a drizzling fall rain soaked the morning grass. His right hand held a half-empty tumbler of Screech on ice as he scowled across the gray water of the barasway at the fog-laden peak of Gun Hill. On the occasional table beside him lay a copy of the Harbour Breton *Coastliner*, and he didn't like what he'd read. He cursed that newspapers could print whatever they wanted. *Too much power, that was the whole trouble. They made people and they ruined people, whatever they saw fit to do. It wasn't fair*!

Worse, he knew this story wasn't even the *Coastliner's*. The editor had copied it from the *News-Advertiser*. It was nothing less than un-Canadian in his mind, and if it wasn't illegal it ought to be. Original stories only. Hard-nosed accountability, that's what newspapers needed.

To his mind, he'd never been given the credit he deserved, and he was certain the editor routinely combed the wire looking for bad press about him just so he could reprint it in the *Coastliner*. The *News-Advertiser* had all but accused him of planting coyote getters and implied that he'd killed two men because of it. And there it was in the *Coastliner* today. He cursed out loud at the press, then he cursed again as he thought about the damage this might do to his predator-hunting bill and even his reputation. He worried he might never carry his riding again.

His mind lashed out. *Why me and not those damned Indians? They've practically ruined this place but the newspapers never print anything bad about them! What the government ought to do is close that reserve and ship them all back where they came from. Peter Joe included.*

Sullivan swallowed the last of the Screech and glared at the window. He wondered why he hadn't heard from that old client. As for the coyotes and wolves, he reminded himself that if he just kept doing what he was already doing every one of them would be gone very soon.

19

I climbed the three steps onto the small wooden porch and knocked on the door of the home of Mark and Myra John, one of a small cluster of homes along a graveled lane beside Little Looe Cove. Their attic and outdoor lights were on, and I knew they would stay that way for the rest of the year while their loved one's spirit journeyed to the Next World. I thought of my father, who'd made the same journey one year ago. I still feel the grief of his passing, yet I also still feel his presence.

It was Myra who answered. Her usual long, black braids had been shorn off in grief. She stepped out and let the door close softly behind her.

"Kwe', Saqamaw Joe. We are honored. We heard what happened at the administration Building today. Are you and the others well?"

"Kwe', Myra. It's kind of you to ask. Yes, everyone is well. Just some broken glass and a bruised ego."

"It seems so very strange. Any idea why or who?"

"No to both of those questions, I'm afraid. But Clarence is on it."

She nodded with a look of relief on her face. "That is good to hear. So, then, what brings you to us?"

"I come to offer my condolences again and to ask how you and your family are coping. And to remind you that help is available whenever you ask."

She sighed. "Wela'lin, Saqamaw Joe. It has been nearly two weeks and we are only a little better. It is still very difficult. He was our rock, and our memories of him are strong. His passing has left a great emptiness in our family."

I nodded solemnly, knowing exactly what she meant.

"He was everyone's rock, Myra," I replied. "Each of us feels his loss very deeply. Many at the Salite told me how much they honored and respected him. But he is with the Old Ones now. He is a grandfather for all of us. "

She nodded with a smile that seemed to hint at a memory. "E'e, Saqamaw. Wela'lin. Your words are kind."

"Weliaq, Myra."

I paused for a few seconds before I spoke again, letting whatever memory she was having linger just a little longer for her.

"I've come especially to check on Mickey," I said at last. "I know his grandfather's passing was especially hard on him. How is he?"

Myra sighed again. "A little better. He leaves his room to eat with us now, but he still blames himself. He doesn't speak, and he returns immediately afterward to his room. I believe a long time will pass before he recovers."

I considered that. What I was about to ask could be an unwelcome imposition at this time in their grief. Yet it could also save the lives of many, including those of our people, and ease the pain of Leon's death, especially for Mickey.

"Do you think he might sit by the river with me for a little while?" I asked. "My father's passing was a great loss for me, just as his grandfather's passing was for him. My father gave me something that helped me remember that life continues even as we lose those very close to us. I hope it will help Mickey, too."

She considered my request for long seconds. "I am hesitant, Saqamaw," she said at last. "We have tried all we can. None of us can reach him in his sadness."

Her gaze drifted to the floor of the porch between us, then she looked up and studied my eyes. "But perhaps it is worth a try," she said at last. "And if he is willing, I will walk with him to the river before I leave you alone together."

"That will be perfect, Myra. Should I wait?"

"Yes, I will ask him now." She went back into the house.

I turned toward the midafternoon sun as I leaned against the handrail. A clattering V of Canada geese flew southward toward a bank of clouds beginning to grow over the strait. A light breeze arose and shook loose a few fall leaves that had already lost their grip. I reflected on how much I loved everything about this reserve.

The door opened several minutes later and I turned back around. I was surprised to see Mickey standing in the doorway beside Myra with her hand on his shoulder. He stood with his hands in his pockets and stared at his shoes.

"Mickey, Saqamaw Joe would like to talk with you," she said.

He didn't respond.

She tried again. "He has something important to tell you, Mickey. Would you like to go with us to the river?" He still didn't respond.

I knelt down onto one knee in front of him. "Mickey, a long time ago my father gave me a gift, a gift that has become very special to me. He can't be here with us now because he passed away last year, but I know he would want you to have it, too."

I waited for him to respond. I was just about to give up when without looking up he nodded his head, just once.

Myra seemed surprised. "I think that's a yes," I said.

With that, we strode in silence down a dirt path to the Conifer River. On the shore we found a small wooden fishing boat overturned by its owner. The three of us sat on its stern and looked out over the river together.

Myra put her hand across the back of Mickey's shoulders, pulled him toward her, and spoke to him softly. "I will leave you with Saqamaw for a little while, Mickey. You'll be safe here. You and Saqamaw can talk." Then she kissed him gently on the forehead and left us. To my surprise, Mickey did not attempt to follow her.

For a long time we just sat together in silence, he head down with his arms wrapped across his waist and pushing at the rocks with his feet, me looking out across the peaceful flow of the Conifer to the tree-covered mount of its northern bank. Halfway across, an eagle flew low over the Conifer's surface. Mickey looked up briefly to watch it pass, then returned his eyes to the ground. I let the silence between us linger a bit longer before I leaned forward, folded my hands, and laid my forearms on my knees.

"Before I was born," I began gently, "my father abandoned my mother and me on this reserve. Before he knew me, before he even looked on my face. Never in my thirty-five years had he ever made an effort to see me, to know me, or care for me. I didn't understand why he left and as I grew older I became angry. Angry at him, but angry at myself, too. I blamed myself that he ran from us, that somehow his knowing I was coming drove him away.

"But by then something wonderful had happened. My godfather, the chief of our people at the time, stepped into his place. And for fifteen years he and my mother stood by me, raised me to be a man, and gave me everything they had to give. I loved them both for it, but especially that he would step in to be the father I otherwise wouldn't have had.

"More than anyone else, he taught me our customs, our beliefs, and our spiritual ways. How to hunt and to fish, how to be with my family and with the family of all our people. How to live as a man, and what it means to be Mi'kmaw.

"And with him I grew to love this place. We often sat in peace together by the sea, in the mountains, or by this river, just as you and I are doing now. We sat and watched nature do what nature does, at its own pace, without interference. That is how I came to understand myself, our people, and what we mean when we say 'Msit No'kmaw.'

"For fifteen years I'd lived here, and I believed that I would always be here. Then, I was taken away. Away to a strange city without peaceful rivers to sit beside, without mountains to walk among, without solitude and quiet. And I was angry again. Angry that my mother would do that to me, angry that my godfather did nothing to keep me here, angry at myself that I could do nothing to stop it.

"Gradually, I came to accept my fate. My mother showed me that I could do well in the white man's school, and I learned to thrive there, too. Gradually my anger cooled.

"Then, just as I was about to reach the highest of educations in the white man's school, a telephone call came. It was my godfather. He begged me to return, almost twenty years after I had left this reserve. And when I did, I learned that he was dying. And again I was angry. Angry that he was leaving me for the second time. But just as much, I was angry at myself. I watched him die in the hospital and I could not help him. I could do nothing to save the man that had given me everything without ever asking for anything in return. And I blamed myself.

"It is said that behind every pain is a blessing. And for me that has proven true, I have had many of each. Even my godfather's passing brought with it a blessing, for it was only then that I learned that he was actually my true father and that I was the true son of a chief. Even in death he looked after me."

I paused to let that last thought sink in. Then I turned my head and spoke to him directly.

"We are taught that we must no longer speak the name of those who leave us to be with the Old Ones. But, Mickey, you can honor your grandfather as he honored you and hold him close in your heart as he held you in his. You and your grandfather, you were born of the same spirit guide, the same direction, and the same color. His blood flows deep within you. He died before you were ready, but not before he taught you everything he could. That's the gift he gave to you, Mickey, the same gift my father gave to me before he died. And I believe your grandfather would want you to open your heart so that you may give that same gift to your family, to your friends, and to all of our people."

I ended there, and he was still for a long time. Then, without warning or sign that anything was about to change, tears rushed from his eyes and he burst into an uncontrollable cry. He buried his head in his hands. His body began to shake.

"I killed my niskamij!" he cried out. He threw himself into me. I held him while he shook and sobbed.

"No Mickey, you didn't kill him." I tried to comfort him when he began to relax. "It was an accident. You didn't know what you found, and neither did he. There's never been such a thing in our forests before."

Gradually he stopped crying. He sat upright, wiped his eyes with his hands, and looked at me with a sniffle.

"But what . . . what was it?" he asked.

"I'll show you." I removed the two photos from my pocket and unfolded them onto my lap. The first showed the coyote getter still buried in the ground.

"That's it!" he said. "It blew some sticky white stuff into his face when I kicked it! He ... he fell onto his back so I ran back to get my dad. But when we got back . . . my niskamij, he . . . he was dead." He started to tear up again.

"It was a poison, Mickey. Someone put it there to kill coyotes and wolves. But that someone didn't stop to think that it could kill other things, too. Even people."

He sniffled again. "S . . . so . . . it wasn't my fault?"

"No, Mickey, it wasn't. In time, you'll come to truly understand that."

He seemed to think about that for a few moments, then drew in a stuttering breath. I hoped he was beginning to accept my words.

That was when Myra returned. "He's been crying," she said with a worried look as she approached. "Is he okay?"

I put my hand on Mickey's shoulder and smiled at him, but I spoke to Myra. "He'll need more time to truly understand but, yes, I think he's eventually going to be fine. I'll ask Mary Benoit, our healer, to spend time with him."

Mickey looked back at me, then turned to his mother. "He said it wasn't my fault, Mom."

She sat beside him and pulled him close. He hugged her back. "He's right, Mickey, it wasn't. It was never your fault."

They sat quietly with arms wrapped around each other for almost a minute, then Myra turned to me. "Wela'lin, Saqamaw. We are indebted to you."

"And I to him," I said. "He's a brave young man."

She spoke to Mickey again as he looked into her eyes. "Come, it is almost dinner time and our family is waiting for you."

We stood and I watched them walk hand-in-hand up the trail. When they had gone, I turned back and looked up at the sky. The sun had begun to beat back the encroaching clouds. "Wela'lin," I said to the sun. I looked out over the broad expanse of the Conifer. "Wela'lin," I said to the river. A breeze rose in my face and shook the leaves, then died again. *Weliaq*, it seemed to say.

I picked up the photos and studied them once again. A device that couldn't kill a man had in fact killed at least one man, most likely two. And not with cyanide powder, but with sticky white stuff. Mitchell and Clarence needed to know that right away.

20

A fully-uniformed Mitchell Gregg, day bag in one hand and jacket in the other, entered the front door of the Hotel Corner Brook and stood facing the historic wall plate behind its admissions counter: HUMBER HOUSE, 1925. He set his bag on the floor, his coat on the bag, then rang the call bell sitting on the counter next to a pot of fresh daisies.

A man in jeans and a plain brown shirt soon approached from a room behind the wall. "Afternoon, Mr. Gregg."

"H'lo, Saul. Hopin' you got a room. No reservation this time—been kinda in a rush. An' it's personal business today."

The manager fingered through a box of index cards on the shelf below the countertop, then pulled one out and studied it briefly.

"Your lucky day. One left."

"Sign me up."

"Very good. Number 307."

Mitchell completed the registration card, which the manager accepted in exchange for the room key. "You remember the routine," he said.

"That I do. Thanks, Saul."

"Pleasure as always, Mr. Gregg."

Mitchell picked up his coat and bag and climbed the stairs to the floor above. At the first door around the corner, he twisted his key into the lock and pushed the door open with his shoulder. He dropped his bag and coat in the corner, pushed off his boots, and threw himself onto the bed, exhausted.

Only this afternoon had he learned that intern Lucie Headley had been involved in a serious accident. He had just driven nearly three hours, knowing nothing about her condition and almost nothing about the accident. *How badly was she injured? Is she even still alive? If she is, will she walk again? Did her parents know? Will she recognize me when I walk into her hospital room a few minutes from now?* He could answer none of those questions.

He swung his feet onto the floor and rubbed his eyes with the heels of his hands. He tapped Google Maps. His previous stays had always been on official business—conducting spawning surveys on the Humber, studying red fox or moose or black bear populations, checking hunting and fishing licenses. But none of that had given him a familiarity with the local streets.

His black Toyota T100 was already old but it still ran like a well-tuned symphony, and the dual exhausts he'd installed two years ago now burbled softly at idle. After letting traffic clear, he let the truck's assuring rumble start him on his way. The phone guided him onto Brookfield Avenue where he turned left into the hospital parking lot. He walked under the hospital's gray concrete overhang and through its double doors to the information desk.

"Afternoon, sir," he said to the aide behind the counter. "Lookin' for Lucie Headley. Came in two days ago. Accident near Steady Brook."

"Lucie Headley, you say?"

"Yes, sir."

The aide perused a computer screen.

"I'm sorry, sir, I don't find that name in our system. Let me try another approach."

A minute passed while the aide tried again. "Well, I'm still not finding her here. Could she instead be at one of our sister hospitals, maybe Stephenville or Deer Lake?"

Mitchell was about to answer when a woman in a white coat approached him from nearby. "Pardon me," she interrupted, "I couldn't help overhearing." She offered her hand to Mitchell. "I'm Dr. Lachalle. Did I hear you mention an accident near Steady Brook two days ago?"

"Mitchell Gregg," he said, returning the handshake. "And yes, you did."

"Young woman, maybe 25 or so, long dark hair and green eyes?" she asked.

"Sounds right. She here?"

"Thank goodness," Dr. Lachalle responded with a sigh. "She was unconscious when she arrived, no belongings, no ID. I've been trying to identify her and locate her family. She came to us with a concussion, facial cuts, and some internal bleeding. She's strong, but she'll need to stay a few days longer before she can be released. She transferred out of critical care just this morning, and I was waiting for her to come out of sedation to find out who she is. It seems RCMP misfiled the records of her accident. Are you family?"

"Not exactly," Mitchell answered. "Family's in Saskatchewan. I'm her supervisor here until her internship is over." His voice broke a little. "Lucie Headley's her name. How is she?"

"She had us worried at first, but she's improving. She's been given a private room and she should be waking up by now. She'll be resting, but you could spend a few minutes with her."

Mitchell relaxed. "I'd like that."

Dr. Lachalle turned to the aide at admission desk. "Try patient name Unknown Steady Brook 9-12."

The aide turned to his computer and scrolled through patient names beginning with U. "There it is," he said at last. "Room 418, fourth floor, Intensive Care."

He slid a register log toward Mitchell and handed him a pen. Mitchell filled in the blank spaces and took the visitor pass visitor pass offered him and clipped it to the zipper of his coat.

"Thank you ma'am, sir," he said, shaking each of their hands. "Might sound silly, but ... well, she's away from home and I feel responsible. For her, I mean. If you know what I mean," he fumbled.

Dr. Lachalle responded with a smile and put her free hand on Mitchell's shoulder. "No need to explain, I understand completely," she said. The aide nodded sympathetically. "Likewise," he added.

Mitchell hurried to the elevator. The door opened immediately revealing two other passengers. The fourth floor button was already lit, so he quickly moved to the back of the car. The door closed and the elevator began to move upward. He rocked on his heels with a nervous feeling in his stomach.

The car door opened and Mitchell followed the other two passengers out. He turned right, followed the zig-zag of hallways until he found Intensive Care, and made his way to the door marked 418. It was partially open. He peered through the crack, then nudged it open a little further.

The young woman on the bed slept with her head turned slightly away from him. The face bandage made it hard to see, but he was sure it was Lucy. She wore a gray-striped hospital gown, and the top of the bedsheet lay over her chest and under her arms. An IV tube ran from a stand on the far side of the bed to the crook of her elbow.

He stepped cautiously inside and stopped just past the door. The room felt warmer than the hallway. “Lucie?” he asked quietly.

Slowly, the woman’s eyes blinked open and she turned her head toward the voice. They blinked several more times before she recognized him. “Mr. . . . Gregg?” she whispered out.

He slid a chair from the corner of the room over to the bed and sat facing her. He smiled gently as he leaned forward and placed his hand on her forearm. “Glad you’re okay,” he said. “I was worried. You’re missed at the office.”

A faint smile blossomed on her face.

“But take as long here as you need,” he added. “I’ll phone your parents, let them know you’re safe.”

She strained to speak and her “Thanks, Mr. Gregg,” came out with a squeak. Then her eyes looked away as if she was trying to remember something. Her smile gave way to a look of worry and her gaze returned to Mitchell. “The . . . samples?”

“Quite a story there, Lucie, tell you when you’re back. They’re in good hands now.”

She smiled at his answer, but said no more and her gaze began to drift again.

“You need your rest, Lucie. I’ll step out now an’ check on you later.”

Her smile remained, but her eyes had already closed and she didn’t answer. He patted her hand and gave her one last look before he moved the chair back to its corner. He left the room and gently pulled the door after him, being careful not to snap the latch.

21

I found Mi'kmaw Police Chief Clarence Paul parked beside St. Anne's School in his patrol car, head down as if working on paperwork. My rap on the driver side window startled him out of his concentration. He looked up, rolled the window down, and hung out his elbow.

"Weli eksitpu'k, Chief," he said.

"Weli eksitpu'k, Chief," I replied.

"Word is you've been making a target of yourself."

"Not by choice." I handed him the note from the rock that had been thrown through my office window.

"Yeah, I heard about this. The guy was headed north so I followed a hunch, passed the description on to Sam at the Dashwood. Maybe he'll get a license number if the crook is dumb enough to stop there for a fill." He held up the note between his index and middle fingers of one hand. "I'll hang onto this in case RCMP can make use of it."

I nodded. "Thanks, Clarence. Maybe they'll give us a piece of this puzzle. It's getting bigger by the minute."

"Meaning what?" he said.

"Meaning I got some new information about our Elder."

"I'm all ears."

"Sticky white stuff."

He pulled off his cap and lazily scratched his head. "Sticky white stuff. There must be more to that."

I brought him up to date on all that I had learned—that Mitchell, Emma, and I had found the same coyote getters where both men had died; that Mitchell Gregg had explained that when bitten by the animal attracted to their scented bait, the getters blow sodium cyanide powder into the face and mouth of their target; that it seemed someone was willing to kill us to protect their secrecy; and that Emma had learned RCMP was also aware of them and has an active investigation underway into their possible relationship to the death of Armless Man.

"Rod Penny," he injected, "RCMP ID'd him to me and other law enforcement agencies, wanted to know if we knew anything about him. Twenty-year-old kid from Badger. Battled with drugs, just left home one day. Parents were devastated when they got the news."

"So tragic, people really struggle sometimes." I mused. At least there had been a family to mourn him; his spirit would pass on peacefully.

"It surely is. But you said cyanide powder. Powder, not sticky white stuff."

"Exactly," I responded. "I spent time with Mickey John yesterday. He's the only one who saw what happened to his grandfather."

"Mickey opened up to you? We got nowhere, he wouldn't even talk to his family."

"He was sure he'd killed his own grandfather," I said. "He was shouldering a man-size pain, and he broke down hard."

Clarence lowered his eyes and shook his head. "So that's why he disappeared. Poor kid, I had no idea he blamed himself." He looked back up. "What did he tell you?"

"Remember that reporter, Emma Walsh? I showed Mickey one of her photos of the getter she and I found, and he recognized it as the same thing he found when he and his grandfather were in the Bay du Nord. He said it blew sticky white stuff into his grandfather's face. And he was clear about that. He hadn't told anyone about that until yesterday."

Clarence nodded. "And where does that leave us?" It came out as a question, but his face told me he was already forming the answer.

"Mitchell Gregg says getters normally won't kill a man—that there's not enough cyanide powder in them to do that. But Mickey made it clear that one of those getters did just exactly that. So there's something different about the ones we're finding. I think there's something other than cyanide in them . . ."

"Something more lethal," he finished for me. "Which could mean involuntary manslaughter, or maybe second-degree murder."

"That's my guess, too."

He thought for a while. "So that changes things. One of our own was killed, and that gets us cred with RCMP and a bit of a hand in their investigation. Sounds like they screwed up the first time around with him. That'll be my first call this afternoon. My second'll be to our attorney, and I expect he'll want to exhume the body."

That last thought struck me hard. Between losing our Elder and watching Mickey withdraw so completely into himself, the John family had already suffered so much. Asking permission to exhume his body would invite even more pain. I worried especially about Mickey, that he'd punish himself again. Or worse.

This was also a spiritual matter. Exhuming his body could break the path to the Next World. His spirit might remain forever in limbo. Yet I knew that Clarence was right. The law would require a conclusive link between the coyote getter and his death. That connection might be the only way to protect the rest of my people from a similar fate, and at the moment I could think of no other way to make it.

I asked myself what my father would have done. How would he have resolved this conflict of earthly and spiritual matters? How would he have justified asking for the unaskable? The answer came almost immediately.

"If it comes to that, I want to know there was no other choice," I said. "And if it does, tell him I want to be the one to make that request of the family. If our Elder's body has to come up, I want them to know that it's the only way to protect others from the same fate. If it's painful for them, I want them to have someone to blame for it and I want that someone to be me."

"Understood," he said. "And I'll make that my recommendation. Best the Johns hear it from someone they trust."

A feeling of relief calmed me inside. "Thanks, Clarence. I owe you one."

The hint of a grin grew onto his face. "You mean one more, Chief."

I chuckled. "But who's counting, right?"

He put on his cap and started his engine, then turned back to me. "Apparently, neither of us," he said, still smiling. "I'll get back to you with our lawyer's advice."

"I'll be waiting."

* * * * *

Mr. S entered the small, run-down, windowless storage shed that he'd convinced its owner to keep for just another year and allow him to use for a purpose he did not explain.

A steel workbench lined one wall, and on it were stacked the boxes and cans of his supplies. Beside them stood a turret-style reloading press. Next to the needle-nose and slip-joint pliers on the shelf above sat a box of nitrile gloves, a full-face respirator, and two boxes of activated-carbon filter cartridges. A Tyvek body-suit hung from a hook beside the door.

He'd acquired most of the supplies quite easily: springs, spikes, lock rings, pistons, and trigger rods could be found online from a variety of suppliers; 'Capsules' was his shorthand for the empty .38-caliber pistol cartridges he could purchase from any number of sporting goods or reloading outlets; scent could come from any merchant of trapping supplies; and narrow strips of red cloth for the wrap and the thread to hold it in place could be found almost anywhere. But the toxin was a different matter. Discretion required that he buy it on the dark web where it commanded a very high price.

His first attempts to squeeze a half dozen drops of the toxin into a capsule with an eyedropper had been clumsy and awkward. The respirator and its two cartridges had put an unfamiliar weight on his face, made it difficult to breathe, and blocked part of his vision. The suit had made him too warm and the respirator slid down his face as he began to sweat. He'd worried the candle flame would ignite the suit while he sealed the top of the capsule with a thin layer of wax. Several times he'd missed the capsule altogether. Twice a capsule had fallen off the bench when he'd brushed it with the loose fabric on his forearm. And one time his legs had spasmed for hours after he'd cross-threaded a respirator cartridge. 'Sub-lethal exposure' is what they'd called it on the website he'd found.

Loading and sealing the capsule had become easier after he'd cut holes in the wall to let fresh air in and built a jig to hold the capsule in place and steady his hand. Eventually, he'd become adept enough to prepare a large number of the devices in just a few hours.

Today, he'd already placed the meticulously-prepared capsules in in a box in sparse layers separated by generous amounts of cotton batting. On top of them he'd placed the stakes in their cardboard sleeves, and a Ziplock bag containing the gauze, thread, and a bottle of scent. All remaining airspace had been firmly packed with bubble wrap. Then he'd sealed the box with packing tape.

He carried the box outside and secured it in the trunk of his car. As he prepared to drive to the meeting place, he thought about the foolish error that had killed his first employee, and the first time he'd met his newest. He'd been put off by the new employee's stutter and he'd questioned his mental capacity. But it had been hard to find someone he could rely on to keep secrets and not ask questions, qualities he considered more important than not making deadly mistakes.

22

I wandered back to my office and found that the broken glass had been cleaned up and a sheet of plywood now covered the window. I made a note to give Lisa, Dave, and Millie special mention at our next council meeting for both their bravery and their thoughtfulness. Every day reminded me that I was only the chief, that the work of everyone else on this reserve is what keeps it going. Sometimes, I wondered why they need a chief at all.

I decided to call Mitchell—he needed to know what I learned from Mickey John, too. I dialed his cell number but got no answer. I left him a message to call me as soon as he could.

I left the building and walked to Loppy's Landing for coffee and to buy a little time to sort things out. When I returned, Mitchell was standing beside my door.

"H'lo, Chief."

"Well, that was fast," I said as I opened my door. "The department must have issued you a jet. I called only twenty minutes ago and you're already here. Come in."

He chuckled. "Well, I was sort of in the area. Thought I'd drop by, see how you're doin'." He slung his coat over the back of my side chair and sat. I sat at my desk.

"In the area?" I asked.

"Yeah, busted a poacher across the bay. Area's been closed to caribou hunting for years now, tryin' to build up the herd there. But that didn't bother him any. One of my guys—posin' as a woodcutter—found the guy's truck near Kikupegh Lake with a bull in his bed. Big one, too. Turns out he lives in Swanger Cove . . . or did until now. On his way to a holding cell today.

"Anyway, word travels fast 'round here." He tipped his head toward where the window used to be. "Looks like you had a little incident."

"You might say that."

"No idea who?"

"None. But this makes me think I've been the target all along—that I'm the one they're after. Maybe you and Emma just happened to be in the wrong place at the wrong time."

"Hmm, could be, I s'pose."

"Anyway," I continued with a sigh, "there's something else I haven't told you yet."

"Like?"

"Like sticky white stuff." I brought him up to date on Mickey's story.

Mitchell appeared to contemplate that. "I don't get it—" he began, but we were interrupted by the ring of my desk phone. I studied the caller ID.

"If this is what I expect, you'll want to hear this, too." I punched speaker and slid the phone between us. "Hello, Anna."

"Hello, dear Peter! How are you?" came the response.

Mitchell's brow rose. "Dear Peter?" he mouthed at me.

"Very well, and you?"

"I am excellent as well. But I must tell you I hear a bit of noise on the line. Perhaps our connection is not good?"

"No, it's fine, Anna. I had a hunch what this was about when I saw it was you, so I put you on speaker. I'm sitting here with Mitchell."

"Ah! Bon Jour to you as well, Mitchell!"

"H'lo, Annamarie."

"Are you calling with what I think you're calling about?" I asked.

"Yes, I am. And it is good that I can inform Mitchell at this time, too. My analysts have given me preliminary results. Still to be verified, of course, but I felt you should know of our initial conclusions immediately."

"We're all ears here," I responded. Mitchell looked away and down at the floor.

"Very well. I will begin with the samples of caribou and eagle tissues which I received shortly after you delivered the coyote getters. Mitchell, I believe your intern had suspected a toxin of some sort would be found in those samples when she collected them. And she was correct, the carcass was indeed tainted.

"Her samples from the eagles' crops, proventriculi, and gizzards will be the most convincing evidence of direct ingestion, and hence the most conclusive proof of cause of death, particularly when combined with expert testimony on the toxin itself. My analysts found the very same toxin in both the caribou and the eagle tissues, so it is our preliminary conclusion that the eagles indeed died from ingesting pieces of the tainted caribou carcass.

"What is significant, as you will come to see, is that the carcass had not only been tainted, it had been tainted with one of the worst toxins one might imagine."

"Do you know what it is?" I asked.

"Yes, and I will get to that in a moment. I want first to address the devices you gave to me, Peter—the coyote getters. As you had described to me earlier, the active end of the device—the 'capsule' as I understand it is called—was wrapped in simple medical gauze. The bait appears to be a fish oil of some kind. We can perform further analyses to determine more precisely what it is, but I suspect that this particular analysis would not be a worthwhile investment for you since it is unlikely to be the source of harm."

"Right, Annamarie. That would be the attractant," Mitchell interjected. "Stuff that draws the coyote to it."

"Oui, Mitchell, that makes sense. What may be more in your interest is the contents of the capsule itself. It contains no sodium cyanide powder as you thought it might. It is instead a mixture of several components, one of which we have not completely identified but which appears to be condensed milk."

"Sticky white stuff," I murmured.

"Correct, Peter, that is its texture. But that product seems only to be the carrier. The toxin it carries we have identified to be what has come to be known as compound 1080."

"Compound 1080?"

"Oui, that is its common name. It is more correctly known as sodium monofluroacetate. And what is significant for your investigation is that it is the very same toxin we found in the carcass and eagle samples."

"And what the hell is it?" I asked.

"A highly effective inhibitor of cellular metabolism," she responded. "The cells of our bodies require energy that helps us to move, breathe, think—and to stay alive. They make that energy themselves in a process biologists call the Krebs cycle. It is a highly complex set of biological reactions, and it is constantly in operation in each and every cell in our bodies, even while we sleep. If it is interrupted for any significant period of time, the cells are starved of energy and they die.

"One of the very critical components necessary for the Krebs cycle is what is known as citrate. Now, If we are exposed to 1080 in a way that allows it to enter our bodies—for example by inhalation or consumption—it is metabolized into what is known as fluoro-citrate. What makes 1080 so effective as a poison is that fluoro-citrate is biologically similar to citrate, and our cells can be tricked into allowing it inside as if it was the citrate the cell needs for the Krebs cycle. But fluoro-citrate is instead an imposter, and it cannot participate in the cycle. The cells which have admitted the imposter cease to make their life-giving energy and they die. And the now useless citrate accumulates in the blood where it binds up calcium, causing muscles to convulse and then fail."

I glanced at Mitchel, wondering if he was having as much trouble digesting all this as I was, but he didn't look up.

"Where does this stuff come from?" I asked.

"That is a very long story," she answered, "but it will demonstrate why 1080 is considered to be among the most sinister of poisons."

"Which means what?"

"It means that a mere teaspoon can kill dozens of people. The sodium cyanide you expected I would find would be just as effective in killing its victims, but 1080 has two important differences. First, while antidotes are available for sodium cyanide, no antidote has yet been found for 1080. And second, sodium cyanide most often kills its victim in under thirty minutes. 1080 can take much longer and cause great suffering, although I believe your elder would have died much more quickly due to his age.

"In animals, the journals describe nausea, vomiting, sweating, confusion, and agitation. These are followed by abnormal heart rhythms, muscle twitching and seizures, unconsciousness, and coma. Death is most often due to ventricular arrhythmia. It is much like slowly torturing the animal to its death.

"And it is much the same in humans. The literature reports twenty-two cases of human poisoning, sixteen of which were fatal. But only two of those seem to have been well documented. In one of those cases, a forty-year-old man died after attempting suicide with an unknown quantity of 1080. At the time of hospital admission he was unconscious, had spasms of the eye and muscle, and irregular heartbeat. During his last hours, his muscle spasms and restlessness continued and he frothed at the mouth. His death was determined to be due to respiratory and cardiac failure.

"The other was an eight-year-old boy who had ingested wheat sprayed with 1080. He developed convulsions, vomiting, unconsciousness, and a heart rate near one hundred sixty. He received treatment which saved his life, but sadly he is paralyzed in both legs and will suffer mental difficulties for as long as he remains alive.

"So, with this information now in hand, you and Mitchell must promise to be very careful if you find more of these devices, yes?"

"Absolutely," I said.

"But now I return to your question, Peter. 1080 was used as rat poison in Nazi-controlled territories during World War II. Hitler considered using it in Holocaust death camps but it was determined to be too dangerous for the guards to handle.

"Here in Canada, its use is legal in only two of our provinces and then only for collars baited with 1080 to protect livestock. If 1080 were to be making its way into this province legally, you would easily recognize it. The company dyes it black for safety reasons."

"Which means the 1080 being used by whoever this person is isn't legal," I put in.

"Yes, Peter, that appears to be the case."

I noticed Mitchell had been oddly quiet through all of this.

"Which also means that someone went to a lot of effort to get it," I added. "Why do that when cyanide is apparently easier to get, kills faster, and is safer to use?" I directed that question to Mitchell as much as I did to Anna.

"That, Peter, is anyone's guess," Anna said with finality. No response came from Mitchell as silence filled the room. I decided to press on.

"It's as if someone wants them to suffer," I said. "Despises them so much they're willing to allow anyone or anything that stumbles onto the getters or a poisoned carcass—like our Elder, the eagles, and Armless Man, who we now know to be Rod Penny from Badger—to die an agonizing death."

Mitchell mumbled.

"My apologies, Mitchell, did you say something?" Anna asked.

"I did, Annmarie," he said more loudly. "We got ourselves an assemblyman in this part of the province that some think is doin' just what Chief described. Sullivan's his name—been a thorn in my department's side for years."

"Ah, oui, I am familiar with this assemblyman. He has made himself —how do you say it—notorious in this part of the province as well. Some of my faculty are especially aware. Do you think he is responsible?"

"Can't say—"

"The thing is, Mitchell," I interrupted, "if he's the one doing this, it could cost him his bill and even his seat in the Assembly. Why would he risk it?"

"Dunno. In his nature? Hates 'em? Hedging his bets in case his bill goes south?"

"And what about whoever shot up my window and told me to stay away from whatever I'm supposed to stay away from? You think he had something to do with that, too?" I asked.

Anna broke in. "Peter, did I hear correctly? Someone shot your windows and threatened you? Are you okay?"

I tried to calm her. "Yes, Anna. The window's a mess, but I'm fine. It happened yesterday."

"Oh, thank goodness. I . . . I worried."

I brought us back to the present and spoke to Mitchell's accusation. "Getting back to my question, we don't have proof it's him, right? What we know is two men died after encounters with those coyote getters, you've been shot at, Emma and I have been shot at twice, and four eagles were poisoned. What if it's the guy on the ATV, or maybe someone else?"

"JUST ONE MOMENT!" Anna shouted. "Did I hear that you have been shot at, Peter? And you as well, Mitchell? What is happening there? What else have you not told me? And who is Emma?"

I jumped in. "It sounds worse than it is, Anna. Yes, we've been shot at, but no one was hurt. It was as if the shots were just a message—a message to stay away from something. Like the shots through my window. What you've told us today fills in the gap. We know what that something is now. And Emma is Emma Walsh, a reporter for the *News-Advertiser*. She went with us to investigate the places where we recovered the coyote getters."

"I see," she said. I could hear her relief. "Forgive me again, and thank goodness you are all well."

"Anything else we need to know, Anna?" I asked.

"I believe you now know everything I know about the getters, Peter," she answered. "I must tell you that my final report to you, Mitchell, may differ from these initial impressions, but at the moment I believe what I have told you is accurate."

"Thanks, Anna. We'll talk more later."

"Au revoir to both of you. And promise me you will be safe, yes?"

"You have my promise," I responded.

Goes without sayin', Annamarie," Mitchell added. I hung up.

We sat with silence for a moment. I rubbed my eyes and sighed. "Well, that was very interesting," I said. "I suspected something unusual, but nothing with this degree of malice."

"Yep—" He was interrupted by another ring of my phone. I checked the caller ID as Mitchell went on. "—it's a nightmare."

It was another familiar number. I hit Speaker again. "Hello, Emma."

"Chief Joe, thank God you're there."

"H'lo, Emma," Mitchell chimed in.

"Mitchell, is that you? Good, this is something you both have to hear."

"This is a day for news. We have some for you, too." I explained to her what Mitchell and I had just learned from Anna, and I told her about the damage to my window and the threatening note.

"Damn," she said, "this is really heating up. Who would have guessed? It's gruesome, if you ask me. But I have to say that what you just told me makes what I learned today even more interesting."

"It's hard to imagine how it could get worse," I said.

"Save The Predators will be staging another demonstration. Newspapers, radio, and television stations have been notified. Press attendance will be big. The most curious part is that it will take place tomorrow at one-thirty"

"That's odd," I said. "Why wouldn't the organizer want to give more notice, get more time to draw attention? And would this organizer by any chance be Ross Nelson?"

"It is. And I would have expected that, too, but it appears that he has something special in mind."

"Like what?"

"Surprise."

"How much of a surprise can it be if he's notified all the press?"

"A surprise for anyone that might oppose him—like Sullivan and his advocates. Short notice, broad coverage, no one there but the people he wants. Cunning, if you ask me."

"An' where is this thing gonna happen?" Mitchell asked.

"None of us would have expected where," she answered. "Harbour Breton."

"Sullivan's hometown," I offered.

"I think his plan is to totally embarrass Sullivan, and to have it broadcast across the entire province," Emma added.

I tried to imagine what it would take to embarrass Sullivan.

"I assume you'll be there tomorrow, Emma?" I asked.

"You bet. I intend to get him on the record. An explanation of his methods is overdue. Can I count on both of you to be there, too?"

"I will," Mitchell answered. "I can't do anything about the people he's hurt, but he'll have to answer to my department for what he's been doin' to wildlife." Then he looked at me. "You, too, Chief?"

I hesitated. The purpose of Mi'kmaw justice was to restore peace and harmony. And by that custom, the perpetrator's family must compensate the victim's family for its loss. But Sullivan was not of my people. If he's responsible for the deaths of two men, white law will see that he is punished.

But I'd committed myself to learn how Leon had really died. Maybe knowing that would help the John family find some comfort. And how many more getters were still out there? How many more coyotes and wolves would suffer a cruel and torturous death? How many more people—how many more of *my* people—might still die because of them? *It has to stop, and it has to stop now.*

"Yes," I answered.

"Marvelous!" Emma responded. "I want to interview both of you there, too. Our readers need to know this is not just about coyotes and wolves."

We said goodbye, I touched cancel, and turned to Mitchell. "What do you make of it?"

"Couldn't say." He stood abruptly. "Anyway, I better get goin'. See ya tomorrow, right?"

I nodded.

As he left, I rocked back in my chair and turned toward the plywood sheet covering my window. I wondered what tomorrow would bring. And I wondered why Mitchell seemed so guarded.

23

Short-eared Rabbit played a trick on the other animals. He told Beaver, "The sun will not rise anymore!" Then Beaver told Squirrel, and Squirrel told Chipmunk, and Chipmunk told Skunk. Soon, all the animals prepared for the sun to not shine anymore. Bear ate blueberries to fatten himself, Squirrel gathered nuts. There was no time to play even though it was a bright summer day.

Rabbit thought this was great fun and he hid in the bushes laughing.

Soon Kluscap came. Bear told him, "Oh, Great Kluscap, there is no time for greeting. Everyone must get ready because the sun will stop rising."

Kluscap knew that would not happen so he called a meeting with the animals. All came except for Rabbit.

Kluscap asked Bear, "Who told you this?"

Bear answered, "Raccoon told me." Raccoon said, "Chipmunk told me." Chipmunk said, "Squirrel told me." Squirrel said, "Beaver told me." And Beaver said, "Rabbit told me."

"And where is Rabbit?" Kluscap asked.

Kluscap found Rabbit in the bushes. He grabbed him by the ears and lifted him up. Rabbit yipped as his ears grew very long. Kluscap said, "Now, Rabbit, you will have long ears to remind everyone not to believe your lies."

It was noon when I finished loading up the Kawasaki. I pulled on my coverall and glanced at the sky. Dark clouds hung over Bay d'Espoir and the mouth of the Conifer, and I wondered if I'd be riding through rain. It was still early fall but I could already feel the cold, wet months of late fall and winter lurking behind them.

And I was uneasy. The Old Ones had spoken to me in the night, had given me a warning. Rabbit's long ears. Someone was lying. *Who? And about what?*

At least I now knew why Leon John, Rod Penny, and four Kitpu had died. Someone hated predators so much that they were able to justify to themselves the indiscriminate killing of anything, or anyone, that encountered their devices. "Sullivan," I said out loud to myself. I no longer wondered who would risk everything to eradicate predators in this way, but I worried that more of my People might soon be found dead. I owed it to Mark and Myra John, and especially to Mickey, to learn what I could. I stifled my uneasiness and rode.

The clouds began to thin as I rode inland, and by the time I'd made my turn onto the Bay d'Espoir Highway the sky had cleared. That alone eased my mind and I began to relax. In a little under an hour, I would arrive at the Coast of Bays and Harbour Breton.

As I passed Jipu'ji'j Park, it struck me that it had been the starting point for every discovery in this mystery. And here it was along my path again. I wondered if yet another piece of this confounding puzzle would show itself today.

The next thirty kilometers presented me with long flat stretches of road wooded with tamarack, black spruce, and balsam fir. Here and there I passed through broad barrens covered only in dry grass and scantily dotted with scrub brush barely two feet high. Soon afterward, canyon-like hillsides began to enclose my route and the road climbed and descended steep hills. The tip of Connaigre Bay appeared on my right. The terrain became even more rugged, and water pockets began to litter the side of the roadway, telling me I was fast approaching the Connaigre Peninsula. I crossed the bridge over Great Harbour Bight. Harbour Breton was just ahead.

Emma had not said where the demonstration would begin today, so I rode the long double bend of Canada Drive through Harbour Breton slowly, looking for something that could have been a gathering. I found nothing. I pulled into Jackman's One Stop for gas and a cup of coffee then doubled back through town along Bay d'Leau Drive, continuing my search.

I found them at last in a large vacant lot between the elementary school and the Catholic church. I rode past the gathering, turned into the church's parking lot, and parked to face the crowd next to an old Chevy Suburban. There I turned off my engine, removed my helmet, and watched from a distance.

The organizer had chosen a good place to gather. Quite a few cars could park here and still leave enough room for people to mill about. It offered a peaceful view of the barasway, Rabbit Island, and Gun Hill in the distance.

Only a few people were there when I'd parked, but now more began to arrive. They donned overshirts or coats and hats with the logos and slogans of Save The Predators—the same ones I'd seen nearly a week ago at Awachanjeesh Pond. And there was a logo that I hadn't seen before—People for Conservation. Soon the signs appeared—END THE SLAUGHTER NOW, KEEP IT WILD NEWFOUNDLAND, and MAN IS THE REAL PREDATOR! once again, and a new one—

WE LOVE COYOTES! It seemed the organizer had expanded his reach.

This group of demonstrators was much larger than I had seen at Awachanjeesh, and it continued to grow, now about thirty, as still more cars arrived.

I watched media vans with their satellite antennae gather at the edges of the parking lot. Television crews from Corner Brook, Grand Falls-Windsor, St. John's, and Stephenville. CBC Radio from Deer Lake and Radio-Canada Premiére out of St. John's.

I now estimated the crowd to be about forty people. They talked together in a loose groups until a compact white sedan arrived. They grew silent and attentive as the driver climbed out of the car and walked toward them.

As Emma had predicted, it was Ross Nelson, the same man who had berated me two days ago for not joining his cause. He approached the group authoritatively with a bullhorn in his left hand.

Media people rushed to his side and thrust recording cell phones into his face. Cameras began filming. He spoke to the media for several minutes before abruptly ending his interactions with them and turning his attention to those who had come to support him. As he addressed them, they began to line up two-by-two. He moved to the front of the line and walked them out of the parking area where they turned onto Bay d'Leau Drive, calling out slogans and waving their signs as they went. Some of the media people followed behind while others walked beside or among the marchers, filming and interviewing as they went. The march had begun.

As I looked around, I saw not a single hunter or anyone else that looked like they might offer the marchers some opposition. It seemed that Nelson had done his job well. But I also saw no sign of Emma or Mitchell, and I wondered where they were. *Will they show up?*

I had just decided not to wait when a familiar red Lumina drove into the lot. Emma jumped out quickly, then ran toward me waving her hand.

"Chief Joe! Can I ride with you?"

"Of course. But don't you want to go with the media crowd?"

"No, too many for now. I'll join them when we get where we're going."

"Okay, jump on."

I turned to her after she was on board. "Seen Mitchell?"

"No, I haven't. That surprises me."

"Yeah, me too." I wondered what would prevent him from being here. Yesterday, he seemed so certain he would be. I put the Kawasaki in gear. We followed the marchers close enough to observe, but I did not want to appear to be one of them.

Bay d'Leau was the main residential route through this end of town, but where the marchers started was at least halfway to its end. Still, homeowners came out to the street as they heard the marchers approach, and passersby stopped to watch. Some smiled and waved or called out their support, others just watched. Still others gave disapproving looks, but no one challenged them.

We followed them to the end of Bay d'Leau Drive and turned with them onto Spencer's Brook Road. Unlike the asphalt pavement of Bay d'Leau, Spencer's was a dirt road and the residential area ended at a turnaround only half a kilometer farther. We followed them to the turnaround, but I questioned why Ross Nelson would lead them in this direction when there was so much of Harbour Breton he had ignored. My memory of the road ahead of them was that it was hardly a road at all and that there were no homes on it. It led to the barasway's northern tip, to Big Pond, and to Northeast Arm, and it offered spectacular views across the water to the mountains on its other side. But it was undeveloped and uninhabited, a dirt track more suitable for off-road vehicles than for family cars, and I began to wonder if they had gone the wrong way. Then they stopped and became silent, as if they had come to the same conclusion.

The line of marchers was long, but I could hear Nelson shouting instructions over the bullhorn. And those instructions were to continue along the road in silence. We followed them for another half of a kilometer before they came to a halt in front of a house I hadn't expected to find here. It was an opulent white and brown Queen-Anne-style house with an exquisitely manicured lawn of at least two hectares. It looked vaguely familiar.

As I was trying to remember why, I heard a vehicle pull up behind us. I turned to see the door of a black Toyota pickup open. Mitchell climbed out and Emma waved to him. I killed the Kawasaki's engine and walked over to meet him.

"You're late, party's almost over," I said. I thumbed over my shoulder at the Queen Anne. "That seems to be the last house on their route."

"Afternoon, Chief. Afternoon, Emma," he replied.

There was something unusual about Mitchell. Then I realized that he was wearing jeans, a pullover, and black ballcap. "No uniform today?" I teased.

He let out a subdued chuckle. "Yeah, in the wash."

I suddenly remembered why the house looked familiar. It was identical to a house across the barasway from where we stood. Only one person would have had the audacity to build a house identical to a provincial heritage site.

"It's got to be Sullivan's," I announced. But before that thought could even sink in, Nelson's voice began to boom over the bullhorn. We turned in unison to see him standing on the front porch, the marchers now gathering into a crowd at the bottom of the steps directly in front of him.

I broke into a run directly toward the crowd with Emma and Mitchell in tow. We fought through the crowd of marchers and forced a path through the media to the bottom step. We arrived just as a man emerged from the house. Media cameras began to roll, reporters pushed recording cell phones toward the porch and shouted out questions all at once. Emma held back on the questions and shouting, but she held her own cell phone forward, too. Nelson raised the bullhorn to his mouth, grinned widely, and seized the stage.

"And here he is, ladies and gentlemen!" he shouted. He thrust out his hand in the owner's direction like an emcee welcoming a guest to the stage. "I give you the man who, despite the vast number of problems desperately requiring decisive action by the current Assembly, seeks only to eradicate every predator on this island! The man who even now kills them where they roam! Minister . . . Carson . . . Sullivan!"

I turned to look at the crowd behind me. Marchers booed and catcalled. Signs waved in the air. Cameras snapped photos and filmed video. At the back of the crowd, a man in camouflage seemed to be working his way around it to the side of the porch. *The first hunter coming to take Sullivan's side*? I had thought I might see more of them by now.

At first, Sullivan looked surprised, as if he couldn't believe anyone would have the gall to do what he was seeing on his own front porch. But he soon gathered his outrage and lashed out.

"So, it's de man from Save De Predators . . . again! I guess you don't remember what happened de last time we were together. Firstly, you can stop those false accusations. And den," he shouted, "you can get yourself and all dese useless people who came with you outa here before I call de RCMP!"

Nelson swung his open hand across the crowd behind him. He spoke to Sullivan but it was clear to me he was performing for the media. "Look behind me, Minister Sullivan, and tell me you don't see the cameras, the reporters, the marchers. Do you know why they're here? They're here to hold you accountable. Accountable to them, the citizens of your riding. What they're telling you is they don't want your ill-conceived plan to kill the wild creatures we hold so dear. And they're here to tell you to stop!"

Cheers and hollers arose from the crowd. Signs waved.

"You called them loathsome," he continued when the noise died. "You told us you'd stop at nothing to give them what they deserve. And now everyone knows you've been killing them off for months with your little exploding devices and poisoned carcasses!" His voice grew louder. "Rid yourself of the burden of those two men who died at your hand, Mr. Sullivan! Those loving men with wives and young children who died because of your selfish and thoughtless crime! Confess now, Sullivan! Save yourself!"

More cheers and hollers and sign waving.

Sullivan glared back. "Tsk, tsk, Mr. Smarty Pants, looks like you haven't kept up on your civic procedure. It's a bill, a proposal that's still gotta pass de legal vote of de people's duly elected representatives. That's how we do it in dis province. It ain't law yet, but you got it right that I intend to see it become one!

"And I read de news, too, sonny. Somebody might be killing dose despicable beasts, and I hope dey get every one of them." He raised his voice again. "But it ain't me, so shut up your smart-assy mouth about it!"

Sullivan looked out at the crowd. His face still carried a scowl. His eyes scanned those of us at the front. They settled on Emma. He pointed directly at her.

"And dere's de snotty-nose kid that started that rumor!" he shouted. "Where'd you get your misinformation, missy?"

This time Emma was uncowed. She took two steps up. "Why do you do it, Minister Sullivan? Why do you put those coyote getters in the wilderness? Now the blood of two men is red on your hands!" She pushed her cell phone's microphone toward him.

"What are you, stupid or something?" he retorted. "Think I'm dumb enough to risk everything I've been working at? You got de wrong man, missy, and you better print a retraction, else I'll sue you *and* your stinking paper!"

He looked past her at Mitchell. He scowled and pointed at him. "Dere's your likely culprit! Mr. Department of Fish and Wildlife. Who knows better den wildlife people how those things work and how and where to put them. All just to get more money to be studying them disgusting beasts but never doing anything about them!"

Mitchell looked back at Sullivan and didn't respond. Two men in black ballcaps stepped up beside him. He whispered something to them and they nodded back.

Sullivan's eyes scanned the front row again. He seemed surprised when he saw me, but he collected himself once again. He glared and pointed his finger at me. "Could be him, too! Everybody knows dem Indians, dey just make trouble for de rest of us!" He pushed his face toward me. "Just like dey're fathers did!"

He looked out at the crowd again and shook his finger at them. "Hell, could be any of you, too!" he accused. The crowd booed loudly and bounced their signs in the air.

Sullivan turned his attention back to Nelson. "And you—you're still trespassin'!" He thrust his finger at the air beyond the porch and yelled. "Git off my propity!"

Nelson stood his ground. Sullivan stormed over to him and began yelling up at his face. Nelson yelled back and a heated argument began. Sullivan yelled, "Git off my propity!" again, then shoved Nelson hard with both hands.

Nelson stumbled backward and lost his footing. He tumbled down the steps and into the man dressed in camouflage. The man tried to catch him, but they both fell backward onto the ground. The man stood first, then stooped to help Nelson back onto his feet. That's when I noticed a rifle slung over his shoulder.

Nelson became livid with anger. He spun the man in camouflage around, yanked the rifle from his back, and pushed him out of the way. I saw Nelson aim the rifle at Sullivan. I heard Mitchell yell, "NOW!" as he and two other men fought their way toward him.

Instinctively, I ran at Sullivan. I took him down and covered him with my body. I heard screaming and media people shouting orders. I heard Nelson yell, "Damn you!"

Then came the sound I hoped I wouldn't hear: gunfire. Searing pain sliced my right leg. My eyes suddenly squeezed shut. I rolled off Sullivan and grabbed at my leg, writhing and moaning uncontrollably for what seemed like minutes.

Someone rolled me onto my back. I heard a voice say, "Try to hold still, sir." I felt my hands being pulled away from my thigh and a sudden pressure take their place. I opened my eyes and saw a woman on her knees squeezing my thigh tightly between her hands. “We’re EMTs,” she said when our eyes connected.

A man squatted beside her. He cut my coverall and jeans from ankle to hip and pulled them open. “Through an’ through, femoral hemorrhage,” he told the first EMT. He placed the heels of his hands high on the inside of my thigh and leaned in heavily.

I tried to relax but the pain was strong. I rolled my head to the side to look away and saw Mitchell and a man in a black ballcap pinning Nelson face down on the ground. A third man in a black ballcap had wrestled the rifle out of Nelson’s hands. Media cameras swung wildly from one scene to another. Marchers ducked and scattered in all directions.

I turned my head to look upward again. I watched the first EMT tear gauze and bandages from her backpack. I saw the worried look on the face of the EMT leaning on my thigh. Sullivan just stared at me with disbelief on his face.

Sounds and voices began to jumble in my head. I grew cold and shivered. Images blurred and sounds faded. It became dark and quiet. I no longer felt the urge to breathe. The silver path of the Spirit’s Road appeared above me. My father took my hand and I felt myself begin to float. He pulled me to him and together we rose upward.

24

Faded visions of my people clothed in animal skins drifted toward us. They encircled us. I felt one of them touch my forehead. I heard them chant in a language I did not understand, as if praying in an ancient form of my people's tongue.

"Is this the Next World?" I asked the one with a hand on my forehead. She only chanted in return. I felt my body begin to sway gently, like a baby rocked in its mother's arms. It comforted me and I began to feel warm again.

I turned and looked into my father's eyes. "Is this the Next World?"

"Moque, gwitji'j. Go now. You have much to do," he said. He smiled at me lovingly, then released my hand.

I felt myself fall away. I drifted and tumbled in the darkness. A sudden rush of air swelled my lungs. I felt a hand squeeze my shoulder. I heard, "Chief, you still with us?"

I opened my eyes and squinted at the blurred image of a man. "Mitchell?"

"Thank God, Chief. We thought you mighta left us."

I took a deep breath and exhaled. I tried to fight the fogginess in my head and the pain in my leg. "How . . .?"

"How long were you out of it?" Mitchell finished. "Dunno for sure. Long enough to give us a damn good scare, though."

Someone had laid a blanket over me and I felt something soft under my head. I tried to sit up but the pain was still too strong. I grunted and lay back down. I raised up my head and pulled away the blanket enough to see the blood-stained bandages on my thigh. I felt suddenly queasy and let my head flop back.

The first EMT gave me a reassuring smile. "You're gonna make it," she said. "I gave you something for pain and to help you relax. An ambulance will be here in minutes." I took a few deep breaths and thanked both EMTs.

I heard a second woman's voice. "That was one hell of a gutsy move, Chief." I turned my head to see Emma smiling. "And I'm pretty pleased. I got photographs, recordings, shots of you and Mitchell doing your thing. Damn brave of both of you! I'd be surprised not to see your faces in every newsreel and headline tomorrow. You'll certainly be in mine."

"Thank you, Emma," I said with a groggy smile. I appreciated her enthusiasm, but right now fame was the last thing on my mind.

I was woozy with pain and whatever drug I was given, but I noticed how quiet it was. No shouting, no booing, no signs waving. I bent my head to look around. Media people were gone. Only a few of the marchers remained, and it looked like they were leaving, too. Even Sullivan had gone.

Brain fog was settling in. I wanted to ask Mitchell what had happened but the blurred images of three men walking up to him interrupted me. It looked like two men wearing ballcaps were holding a third man between them. Sounds had already begun to fade, but I heard "mission accomplished," then something about "recognition" directed at me. I saw a vehicle with flashing lights. I felt myself being lifted off the ground. As the vehicle begin to move, I blacked out.

* * * * *

I was awakened by something tugging at my arm and hand. I saw the fuzzy image of a nurse. I fell back into a deep sleep.

When I awoke again, I realized I was in a hospital bed with an IV in my left arm, a blood pressure cuff on my right, a pulse monitor on my finger, and a bandaged leg. It ached. I heard the steady beep of a heart monitor somewhere behind my head. Quiet chatter near my feet caught my attention. I lifted my head and saw two figures through a slowly disappearing haze.

"H'lo, Chief. Glad you're back . . . again."

I managed to collect myself. "Mitchell? Emma?"

"Who else?" Emma replied.

I let my head slump back onto the pillow. "You have no idea how good it is to see the two of you."

"Well, hell, what kinda friends would we be otherwise, right? Glad you're comin' around," I heard from Mitchell.

The brain fog was lifting. What had happened before the ambulance took me away was beginning to come back. "Mitchell ... did I hear someone say 'mission accomplished' back there?"

"You did."

"What was that about?"

"Long story."

"I think I'm gonna be here for a while."

"As am I," Emma added. She had begun to set up her cell phone to record when Mitchell caught her eye.

"But none of it goes to press until *after* charges are publicly released, right?" he said.

She mimicked a salute.

"Okay, then," he said. "Arrests you saw earlier were the end of an undercover job."

"Undercover?"

"Right. Customs, RCMP, Health's Pest Management Regulatory Agency or PMRA as they call themselves, an' my department."

"So, they didn't arrest Nelson for shooting me?"

"They'll charge 'im with that for sure," Mitchell assured me. "But there'll be a whole lot more."

I was stunned. "I'm listening."

"So, 'bout a month ago one of my guys was out huntin' the Bay du Nord when his dog sniffed out a getter. Knew what it was from his days with Alberta Wildlife so he kept his dog away. Brought it back, an' turns out there was somethin' unusual about it. Cyanide getters usually use a plastic capsule, what he found had a pistol shell with a light primer. Shell was filled with white liquid, not the usual cyanide powder. We all expected we'd see illegal cyanide getters here sooner or later, but this one said we were up against somethin' very different.

"About the same time, Customs got a tip about small quantities of 1080 comin' contraband into Canada. They set up surveillance, an' if they found a shipment like that, they'd release and track it. After two to the same address, they knew they were onto something.

"1080 is only legal in Alberta and Saskatchewan, right? So, Customs called PMRA an' PMRA got a warrant. They found the 1080 in a box with what turned out to be a fake name on it, a few coyote-getters, and everything somebody'd need to make more of 'em there. They called me, wonderin' if we mighta seen any getters like that on our rounds. We'd seen only the one up 'til then, but that's when my department got hooked in."

Emma interjected. "So, you already knew what we'd found in the forest together."

"And you already knew what Anna would say when she called to tell us what she'd found," I added.

Mitchell gave us an apologetic look. "Yeah, I did. At the time, we didn't know how big this thing was gonna be. Took us a long time to figure out it was only a small operation. But my behavior musta been plenty confusing for both of you. I apologize for not bringin' you in early on, but the lawyers said it was gonna be a criminal case an' gave us strict orders to keep quiet about it.

"As for Annamarie, always good when somebody else confirms what you think you know."

"So it was Nelson? He was the guy planting the getters?" I asked.

"More or less. He'd been building 'em, but always made his employee plant 'em."

"Why would he do that? His whole thing has been to save the coyotes. He even wanted me to sign on with him." I reflected on that for a second. "Damn good thing I didn't."

"Well, Sullivan bein' who he is doesn't have a lotta friends in the Assembly, right? We'll know more after Nelson's interrogation, but our best guess is Nelson knew that an' hoped someone would accuse Sullivan and the Assembly'd take up an investigation. Investigation like that could take a long time, but there'd be a good chance it'd discredit Sullivan pretty quick even if it later found him clean. Mighta worked if Nelson'd played it out, but things went sideways when he lost his temper."

"Lost it *again*," I put in.

"Right, Chief. An' I 'spect Sullivan's bein' dismissive about him put a big dent in his ego."

Emma looked suddenly terrified. "My God, I got suckered in, too. What an idiot I was!"

"Maybe yes, maybe no," Mitchell answered. "You prob'ly kept Nelson from worryin' about whether anyone was wise to him, and that helped us in the end. But yeah, a retraction might be a good thing."

Emma nodded. "Yep."

"How'd you know it was Nelson?" I asked.

"Didn't for a long time. But yesterday one of my guys out on his rounds came across a fella planting a getter near the western edge of Jubilee Lake. Knowin' about the earlier one, he pressed the fella hard. The fella got pretty nervous but spilled the works on a man he called Mr. S. Agreed to let my guy follow him at a distance to his meeting with that Mr. S, an' that's where my guy recognized him. He'd seen him as Ross Nelson at Awachanjeesh Pond when we were there.

"McCabe's the fella's name," Mitchell continued. "Got a serious disability an' Nelson took advantage of it. He prob'ly had no idea what he got himself into."

"That was the guy in the camouflage today," I conjectured.

"Right. Told us Mr. S, who we now know is Nelson, told him to stand beside Sullivan an' show support. Nelson made sure none of Sullivan's usual supporters knew about the demonstration so Sullivan couldn't steal the show. Our best guess right now is that Nelson wanted McCabe next to Sullivan as somethin' to work up the crowd, boost the jeer factor in front of the cameras. But McCabe didn't get that far before Nelson snapped."

"But if there was no intent on McCabe's part, why'd they haul him off, too?" I asked.

"Well, McCabe's the one been plantin' the getters, so law says he's got some accountability, too. He'll cooperate, but what happens to 'im all depends on the jury."

"And the person taking shots at us beside Little River and Medonnegonix, was that McCabe, too?"

"Yep. Said Nelson told him to make sure to keep what he was doin' secret. I s'pect more will come out when we get the whole story."

"So why did Nelson bother with 1080? Why didn't he use cyanide powder, like getters would normally have?"

"We think he knew Sullivan hated coyotes an' wanted to paint Sullivan as evil as he could to maximize the odds his bill would be shut down. So Nelson went underground for the worst stuff he could find."

"Huh. So, with what Anna told us yesterday you can connect Nelson to the deaths of our Elder and Armless Man, right? What about the eagles?" I asked.

"Armless Man'll be easy, RCMP has his blood work for it already. But not for your Elder."

I thought back to an earlier conversation. "I might be able help with that."

"Then he'll pay for that one, too. The eagles, can't say for sure. But a prosecutor'll know how to get it out of him."

I sighed out loud. "Just astounding. And the shots and rock through my window, how are they connected?"

"Unrelated, turns out. RCMP has the guy. Said Sullivan conned him into scarin' you off, keep you from messin' with his bill."

"But I wasn't."

"Right. But you heard 'im today. Sullivan's's got a thing about Indians bein' responsible for everything bad.

Anyway, my guess is that guy will get jail time for vandalism, an' maybe for assault, too, dependin' on what his intentions were. Sullivan, on the other hand, gets a good deal of protection from parliamentary privilege. The man's a scoundrel for sure, but we'll have to wait an' see what charges are actually brought against him. Nelson was trespassin' when Sullivan pushed him, an' it's all on film."

I had no reason to question anything Mitchell had told us, but it was a lot to take in and the drug was having its effect. "We'd just found the getter where Rod Penny died. And we were talking about this in my office only yesterday."

Mitchell sighed. "Boggles me, too. Things came together fast an' at the last minute. Good example was seein' you yesterday. Pure damn luck. If yesterday'd been any different, I'da missed Emma's call and we'd still be tryin' to figure out how and where to grab Nelson.

"An' that's it," he ended.

My eyes became heavy as I looked from Mitchell to Emma and back again. "Incredible."

"Ditto here," Emma said as she turned off her recorder. "This is gonna make a damn good story . . . after the charges are released, of course."

"Can't wait to read it," I heard as I dozed off again.

25

It was only seven in the morning when Emma Walsh returned to her blue cubicle after making coffee in the break room. For two days she'd been arriving earlier than usual, hoping the news she'd been waiting for had arrived.

She had just sat down in her company-issued ergo-chair when her cell phone issued a quiet *ding:* a text message. It said *Charges filed, M.*, followed by a link to the indictments.

"*Yes!*" On her computer, she pulled up the draft piece she'd created while waiting for Mitchell's word. She made two phone calls, added the final details, then read it for the last time.

WILDLIFE ACTIVIST AND ACCOMPLICE CHARGED IN WILDERNESS DEATHS, INJURY

Emma Walsh, News-Advertiser

Charges filed today in provincial and federal courts blame actions by Save The Predators activist Ross Nelson and accomplice Billy McCabe for the deaths of two men. The men were identified as Leon John, an Elder of the Mi'kmaq Reserve, and Rod Penny,

Nelson's previous accomplice and resident of the Little River area.

An investigation led by agents from Health Canada, Canada Border Services Agency, Newfoundland and Labrador's Department of Fish and Wildlife, and the RCMP culminated in the arrests during a demonstration led by Nelson in front of the home of Carson Sullivan, a resident of Harbour Breton and minister of the House of Assembly for the Fortune Bay-Cape La Hune riding.

Nelson is also separately charged with assault on the lives of two additional men stemming from an altercation between Nelson and Sullivan during the demonstration. Officials allege that Nelson grabbed a rifle from McCabe and fired it at Sullivan. The heroic action of Chief Peter Joe of the Mi'kmaq Reserve saved Sullivan's life when he tackled Sullivan to the ground. Joe was severely injured when the bullet intended for Sullivan struck him in the leg. The quick response of two EMTs who declined to be identified saved Joe's life, and Mitchell Gregg of the Newfoundland and Labrador Department of Fish and Wildlife and his team disarmed Nelson before he could do more harm.

The indictments allege that Nelson illegally imported and used a toxin known as compound 1080 to manufacture predator-control devices known as coyote-getters; that he hired McCabe to place those devices at numerous locations in south central Newfoundland; that no warnings of the presence on publicly-accessible lands of devices lethal to humans and animals were posted; and that such actions caused the deaths of the two men.

While 1080 is used as a predator-control substance, it is also known to be lethal to humans in small quantities. Its importation into Canada is regulated by the Canada Border Services Agency and its use is strictly controlled by Health Canada's Pest Management Regulatory Agency. Licenses limit 1080 to small quantities for use only by the wildlife agencies of two provinces. Newfoundland and Labrador is not among them.

Officials believe that Nelson's intention had been to divert blame for manufacturing and placing the coyote getters onto Sullivan in a move to discredit him and a controversial predator-control bill he had tabled before the assembly.

Other charges against Nelson include discharging a firearm within three hundred meters of a dwelling and numerous violations of provincial wildlife regulations.

Attempts to reach Nelson and McCabe for comment were unsuccessful. A message left by the Save The Predators Halifax office in response to our inquiry said a statement would be forthcoming.

CORRECTION: The *News-Advertiser* apologizes for its implication in a previous article that Minister Sullivan was responsible for the importation, creation, or placement of coyote-getters. That statement was incorrect.

She saved the final version on her own computer, copied it to the work page of the internal server and, with a flamboyant gesture of her index finger, hit send. She smiled broadly, leaned back into her chair, and finished the last of her coffee.

* * * * *

The surgeon had told me I was one of the lucky ones. The bone was intact, but the bullet pierced the femoral artery and ripped a gaping hole through muscles I can't remember the names of. Two hours of surgery removed damaged tissue, sutured torn muscle, cauterized small veins, and grafted big ones. I was told I'll be wearing these bandages for at least a week, using this leg brace for more than a month, and taking antibiotics for nearly as long. She said the numbness from the damaged nerves would go away after a few months.

The still-lingering pain was tolerable, but the thought of climbing the three steps onto the Johns' porch on crutches told me I would need the skill of a tightrope walker. I didn't so I put both crutches under my right arm, left hand on the railing, and hopped up one step at a time on my good leg. I reset my crutches under both arms and rocking-horsed myself to the door. *Success.* I stopped there to rest, then knocked and waited against the railing.

Only a few moments passed before Myra opened the door. "Weli eksitpu'k, Saqamaw. Two visits in four days, we are doubly honored!"

"Kwe', Myra," I answered. "It's nice to see you again."

Her eyes went to the crutches and leg brace and her brow rose. "Oh my, what happened to you?"

"Wrong place, wrong time," I said with a half-smile.

"I'm so sorry to hear that. It looks serious. We'll pray that you heal quickly."

"Wela'lin, Myra. That's very kind of you."

"What brings you to us today, Saqamaw?"

"I have a special request, Myra, and I'd like to talk with you, Mark, and Mickey about it."

"Of course. Piskwa'. I'll get them."

She held the door while I hobbled into their living room, then she called for Mark and Mickey to join us. They arrived from upstairs with five-year-old Rosie in tow and greeted me. Mark asked about my leg, too.

Mark offered me the comfortable looking armchair in the corner of the living room while he and Myra sat side-by-side on the couch opposite me. Mickey sat on Mark's lap and Rosie went to Myra's. I leaned my crutches against the wall beside the chair and pivoted around on my good leg to sit down. Rosie grinned and gave me a child's wave, and I returned her greeting with the same.

"So, how may we help, Saqamaw?" Myra asked.

I paused for a short while, trying to gauge how best to ask the unaskable. Interrupting the journey of a spirit into the Next World would be a matter of high importance, and a personal decision they would have to live with for a very long time. I let out a deep breath.

"Mark, Myra, Mickey, Rosie, the people responsible for your Elder's death have been found and arrested."

Myra gasped and put her hand to her mouth. Mark's and Mickey's eyes widened. "Oh, thank goodness!" Myra said. "What will happen to them?"

"I don't know for sure, but that's why I'm here. I have a very important question to ask you. It may be necessary to perform some special tests to prove to a judge or jury what they did to him. If that's necessary, would you give permission to exhume his body?"

Mark and Myra stared at each other for what felt like a long time, seeming not to know what to say. I offered to give them more time, to come back another day. It had, after all, been little more than two weeks.

They spoke at length to each other in hushed tones. Mark seemed to suggest an answer and Myra nodded to him almost immediately. It was Mark who finally spoke.

"Wela'lin, Saqamaw Joe. We thank you for your kind thoughtfulness, and for being direct. But what you ask would be very difficult for us. He is gone now and his spirit is on its way. We must respect that. We must respect our beliefs, too, and his. So much disturbance in our family these past weeks. It is time we let him go." He sighed. "I'm afraid our answer is no."

I looked from Mark to Myra and back again. Their faces told me they were sure of their decision.

"Very well, then, I respect that. I'll tell Clarence Paul and the attorney that you prefer he not be disturbed. Thanks for hearing me out." I was rising to gather my crutches and say goodbye when I saw eight-year-old Mickey look intently into his parents' faces.

"Mom, Dad, it's okay," he said.

They both turned to him at the same time. "What do you mean, son?" Mark asked.

"My niskamij, he's still here. He talks to me at night sometimes. He said he's stuck. He wants to help other people from getting sick like he did. But he can't. Maybe if we help Saqamaw, that would help those other people, and then my niskamij can go to Next World."

Mark and Myra turned to each other again. A long silence fell between them as they considered Mickey's words. I decided to sit again. Myra's face softened as she nodded subtly to Mark once more. Mark nodded back to her, then turned to Mickey. He put his hand on Mickey's shoulder, squeezed it lightly, and smiled. "So much wisdom in such a young heart." Mickey smiled back.

Mark turned to me. "Well, you heard it, Saqamaw. Permission granted."

Relief passed over me and I rose again.

"Wela'lioq, Mark, Myra ..." I shook their hands. I bent over to shake Mickey's hand. "... and especially you, Mickey. You have been a brave young man. I promise we will do well by your niskamij."

I straightened and told Mark and Myra that they might have to sign some legal documents. I gave Rosie a quick wave, collected my crutches from the wall, and rocked forward. Myra opened the door and I hobbled out onto the porch. I thanked them once more.

The door closed and I turned to face the steps yet again. I assumed that what got me up would get me down, so I repeated my earlier trick, then crutch-walked to the main road and turned left toward the administration building. A few meters later, I heard a car approach from behind so I moved aside. It slowed, then stopped beside me.

"You got a hitch in your get-along there, Chief," said a familiar voice. I turned to see Police Chief Clarence Paul smiling broadly through his open window. "I'm headed back to the admin, need a ride?"

I glanced up and down the road. "Well, I don't see any other offers coming along right now, so why not?" I answered with a grin. He leaned over and opened the passenger-side door while I hobbled to the other side of the police cruiser. I wedged myself backwards onto the seat, pulled myself and the crutches in, and closed the door after me.

"Heard about what you got yourself into," he said. "Been all over police radio. Sounded like a nasty encounter." Then came that grin again. "But you know . . . if you were just tryin' to get a few days off I'da put in a good word for you with the Saqamaw."

"That woulda been too easy."

"I s'pose you're right. So ... fill me in."

"Well, it seems our criminal is Ross Nelson. He and his employee, a kid with a disability that goes by Billy McCabe. The story is they'd been making coyote getters and planting them in the forests, packing them with some chemical called 1080 to kill a bunch of them off. That's what killed our Elder."

"Well, I'll be. But isn't Nelson that Predators fella?"

"Right," I interrupted. "The Save The Predators guy that tried to get me to help him save the coyotes, supposedly. Mitchell said his plan was to make it look like our Minister Sullivan was the culprit, to discredit him and kill his predator-hunting bill."

"Well, about time someone had in mind to put Sullivan out of our misery, but I wouldn't have suggested he do it the way it ended." He pointed at my leg with his eyes.

"I'm with you there. Anyway, one last thing. The John's gave permission to exhume our Elder's body. That should add one more count to Nelson's charges."

"Got it. I'll tell our lawyer to draw up the papers."

The administration building appeared in the windshield. "This good for you?" he asked as we approached the parking lot.

"Yeah. I'm pretty sure things are waiting on my desk . . . that is, unless you took care of them for me while I was gone."

"Good thought, Chief . . . but not likely." He killed the engine. We climbed out of the cruiser and walked toward the entry.

"Thought so. But would you mind getting the door?" I asked.

"Happy to. But unless you need me to carry you, I'm gonna go up ahead."

"I'll be okay. I'll see you later, Chief."

"Right. See ya later, Chief."

The med tech who had fitted me for the brace and crutches had said getting around would get easier with practice, but I decided to use the elevator. I made my way down the hall to my office and laid the crutches on the floor beside my desk. On the desk were four neat piles of paper, signs of Millie's organizational skills, awaiting some kind of response from me. There were only two phone messages so I decided to start there.

The first was from Mitchell. It said he was on his way to Corner Brook and called to let me know that someone from the department would be returning the eagle carcasses to us tomorrow. The second was from Anna. She'd heard from Mitchell Gregg and would I call her right away.

I called Jason about the eagles and asked him set up a reception ceremony. Then I called Anna. She answered on the first ring.

"Bonjour, dear Peter." She sounded worried.

"Hello, Anna."

"Mitchell said I should call. Are you okay?"

I debated what to say. I didn't want her to worry more than she already had. "Yes, I'm okay now," I began, trying to keep it simple. "I saved a man's life. I knocked him down and covered him with my body. It was a rifle; the bullet went through my thigh. Mitchell Gregg and his team disarmed the shooter. The intended victim was our Minister Sullivan."

"Mon Dieu, Peter! I would not have believed it if not from you! It is brave and selfless what you did for a very selfish man. He owes to you his life." She went quiet for a bit, as if thinking. "In my family we have a saying," she continued, "Une vie honorable est une vie éternelle. It means something like doing good things for others makes a forever life. It is sad that you suffer now, but you will be remembered long for your courage and sacrifice."

"Thank you, Anna, that's very kind. We have something like that, too, in our prayer to the Great Spirit of the South. We ask that the strong be also kind, the just be also merciful, and the courageous be also compassionate. I want always to be guided by those intentions."

"And how do you feel?"

"Well enough, I suppose. A little pain still and getting around is awkward, but I manage. I'll find a housekeeper or a friend to help out for a little while. Council business will keep me focused, take my mind away from it."

"Oh, Peter, I wish I could be there to help in some way."

"That would be wonderful, Anna, but the work you do there is very important, too. Young people need you."

"Yes, but it has become a bit tedious. The work of a department chair is often not exciting. I wish to have a change."

"What will you do?"

"I do not yet know, but I am thinking of it a lot. Maybe just some time away, time to think about what I want at this time in my life."

"I think you should do whatever makes you happiest, Anna."

"Thank you, Peter. I will let you know what I decide."

We both went silent until she said, "Well, I must go now. I have much administration to do. Au revoir, Peter. Be well."

"You too, Anna. And good luck with your decision."

I hung up and felt that empty feeling again. The one hour we'd had together five days ago couldn't make up for the year we'd been apart. And now it seemed like it might be even longer. I gave out a long, deep sigh.

* * * * *

The dual exhausts of the Toyota T100 rumbled confidently as it cruised west on the Trans-Canada Highway. Mitchell Gregg took Corner Brook's Confederation Drive exit, turned left on West Valley Road, then right onto Brookfield Avenue to the parking lot for Western Memorial Regional Hospital. He strolled in to the reception desk.

"May I help you, sir?" the attendant asked.

"Yep. Lookin' for Lucie Headley. Been released from ICU."

The attendant typed her name into his computer. "It looks like she's in Room 208 now."

Mitchell gave a mini-salute with two fingers, as if tipping his hat. "Thanks!" He took the elevator and strolled the hallway to 208.

The door was open as he approached. Inside, Lucie stood with her back to the door, putting her personal things into a bag. He rapped on the doorjamb.

"H'lo, Lucie," he said cheerfully. "Ready for that ride back to the office? Lotsa people lookin' to see you again!"

She turned toward him. “Mister Gregg!” She hurried over and hugged him around the neck. “It’s so wonderful—like going home!”

Mitchell blushed, but managed to return her smile. “Road’s waitin’!” he said.

Lucie grabbed the bag and her coat. Together they took the elevator to the main floor and walked to Mitchell’s waiting truck. As he made a left onto West Valley Road, he asked Lucie if her parents had come to visit. “Called ’em the day I first came to see you,” he explained.

“Oh, yes, my parents were here two days ago! It was sooo nice to see them, and they bought me this bag and some clothes. My dad asked me if I wanted to come back to Saskatoon with them. I said no, that I like it here, that Grand Falls-Windsor and the department are my places now, at least for a while. I could see he was a little disappointed, but I think he understood.”

She sighed lightly. “My dad was the one who worried about my happiness the most. I could always count on him to take care of me.”

She turned forward and said nothing for almost half a minute. Then, without looking at Mitchell, she added, “You’re a lot like my dad, Mr. Gregg.”

Mitchell glanced at the side of her face. It carried a soft smile. He looked forward again and dabbed with his sleeve the wetness that had suddenly collected in the corner of his left eye.

26

Early November

MHA Carson aka Hunter Sullivan stood before a three-and-a-half-ton, seven-and-a-half-meter, dark bronze statue on Prince Phillip Drive in St. John's. The man of the statue was Portuguese explorer Gaspar Corte-Real.

Sullivan had often stopped here on the way to his office because he thought himself and Corte-Real to be alike in so many ways. In the mariner captain's uniform of his country and time, Corte-Real stood tall and proud with feet spread wide, arms folded defiantly across his chest, and eyes focused keenly on the horizon. A waist-length sword hung from his belt, and his cape flowed lightly in the breeze as he sailed bravely toward the New World. In his brown and yellow checkered suit with red bow tie, Sullivan saw himself as a courageous mariner of the assembly standing tall at his desk, bringing brave, new ideas to the world, moving them always forward despite the stormy waters of politics that might besiege him at any time.

But today, his likeness to Corte-real held special meaning. Today, he would deliver the final parliamentary speech that would at last seal the passage of his predator-hunting bill.

He placed his hand on the lintel and gazed up at Corte-Real one last time before turning to face Prince Phillip Drive and pushing the crosswalk button. The remains of an Atlantic hurricane that had drenched the seaboard states had brought a cold drizzle to St. John's and darkened the early afternoon sky. He pulled his bucket hat down around his ears and gripped the collar of his mac while he waited.

Four cars and a delivery van later, the lights changed and Sullivan crossed. He took the sidewalk beside the Confederation Building's East Block and turned toward the concrete steps behind the statue of John Cabot. He slowed to admire the eleven-story central tower and its north and south wings, built to house the provincial government after it outgrew the Colonial Building many years ago.

He climbed the steps to the landing and stopped under the awning to shake the rain from his mac. He slung it over his forearm, pulled open one of the tower's glass entry doors, and strode proudly into the building's lobby. There, just as he'd always done on the first day of every sitting, he stopped at its center and basked in the lobby's decor. Provincial employees rushed past him on their way to the elevators as he stood there. But for him this building and this room told him that, as one of the few chosen as Ministers of the House of Assembly, he was a very important man.

His eyes took in the mural by Newfoundland artist Harold B. Goodridge with its scenes and characters of Newfoundland from before and after confederation. He saw images of a Viking at L'anse aux Meadows, John Cabot, former Canadian Prime Ministers Mackenzie King and Louis St. Laurent, a Canadian Mountie, and Newfoundland's first premier, Joseph Smallwood. The Altar of Remembrance with its book of vellum and seal skin commemorating the courageous men and women of the

Royal Newfoundland Regiment who died during World War I's Somme offensive rested on the floor below it.

The images reminded him that in their time those men and women were just common people like him, but common people driven to do great things, just as he would do today. His face beamed and his heart swelled with pride. He was certain his speech before the assembly today would earn him a place on a mural like this for future generations to admire.

He walked to the elevators at the back of the lobby, pushed UP, and waited. Two men approached him from behind as the bell chimed. Sullivan boarded, pushed the button for his fourth-floor office, and stepped to the back of the elevator. He recognized the other two men as members of the Management Commission.

"Mornin', by's. Gonna be a great first day in de Chamber today, eh!" he said with a confident smile.

The two men turned toward the front of the elevator and exchanged barely perceptible smirks. "Sure will, Sullivan. Sure will," said one of them.

The doors opened and all three stepped out. The two Commission men turned left while Sullivan turned right down the hallway toward his south wing office. He fished his keys out of his pocket and unlocked the door. Inside, he hung the wet mac on the coat rack beside the desk. He went to the window wall, drew open the blinds, and reflected on the scene before him.

He longed for a view that took in the great breadth of the city, the Harbour, Signal Hill, and the expanse of the North Atlantic from the highest floor of the central tower. What he saw instead was the roof of the West Block, the massive asphalt parking lot beside it, the winding concrete paths of Allandale Road and the Trans-Canada Highway, and the Pippy Park campground and trailer park.

He turned around. His three-meter square office had been appointed with standard-issue furnishings—an L-shaped wood veneer desk, wood veneer bookcase, wood veneer credenza, and a pair of metal filing cabinets. He mused that none of it befit his stature, that he deserved better. He groaned as he walked to his desk.

He sat in his standard-issue wheeled executive chair and sorted through the documents his staff had left for him early last week. On the very top was a report from the Management Commission to which his staff had attached a hand-written sticky note saying, "Read this."

He scowled. *Another friggin'problem in the House accounting system? Idiots!* He tossed it aside.

Next was the Order Paper, the schedule for today's proceeding. He eagerly scanned the page until he found what he was looking for. It came right after the Management Commission's report:

THIRD READING OF BILL NO. 26
AN ACT TO AMEND THE WILDLIFE ACT, 1990, AS AMENDED.

He beamed again, for today he would reaffirm himself as a true leader of Parliament, a man deterred by neither hardship nor obstacle in his bold mission to serve the people of Newfoundland and Labrador. His speech would be heard live and province-wide on the House of Assembly TV channel and would be forever immortalized in the Hansard. He could already hear the words of the speaker: "This bill having had three separate readings, is it the pleasure of the House that it does now pass?" followed by an echoing chorus of "Aye," standing applause, and raucous cheers of "Hear hear!"

Allowing for the speaker's parade and routine proceedings, he guessed his bill would come up at about two-thirty. Standard procedure called for him to simply read the bill for the third time. At this point in its life, debate was possible but not common and was confined to the bill as a whole. But he decided he'd take that opportunity to elaborate on its benefits to all Newfoundlanders once again. Today would make him a true lawmaker, he was sure of it. And It would be an easy path to province-wide admiration and acclaim from there.

He looked at his watch. *Plenty of time for a stroll to the canteen for a latte and the elevator ride to the ninth-floor Chamber*. He grabbed his copy of the bill and left his office, letting the door slam.

At two twenty-five, he entered the Chamber and closed the door softy behind him. He smiled broadly and nodded to the sergeant-at-arms sitting beside it. Protocol required that he wait until no one was speaking before crossing the center of the Chamber. He bowed as he passed in front of the Speaker sitting at the head of the Chamber in his hand-carved, high-backed chair. He passed the clerks at their table in the center of the Chamber.

His desk sat in the middle of the second row, Opposition side. He put his latte on its corner, leaned back into his chair, and waited for the Speaker to announce his bill. The gleam of the gold-plated sterling silver mace, the Chamber's symbol of the rank and authority, caught the corner of his eye. He had a clear view of its rich imagery: maple leaves, the fishery, the coats of arms of Canada, Newfoundland, British Columbia, and King George VI. And at its very top, a life-size replica of the St. Edwards Crown used in the coronation of Canadian Sovereigns.

From the banter taking place after he sat down, he realized that the House was still mired in oral questions. He looked at his Order Paper. They hadn't even gotten to the Management Commission's Report yet. He huffed inside, but he knew he had no choice but to wait it out.

Ten more minutes passed before questions ended. The Speaker moved quickly to make up time. "Next in Order, the Honorable the Member for Conception Bay South will present the Management Commission's special report," he directed.

The woman sitting just to the right of center on the Government side stood. Sullivan knew her as the Government House Leader.

"Thank you, Speaker," she began. "Mr. Speaker, Honorable Members. Two months ago, the commission received a complaint with supporting information from members of the public regarding the improper use of public funds by this Chamber. Shortly thereafter, the bipartisan Management Commission undertook a special investigation of that complaint. Today's report concludes that investigation and alleges certain breaches of privilege and contempts of the House—" Murmurs arose among the members, and she paused.

"Order, please," the Speaker reminded.

"Somebody gonna be in trouble," Sullivan whispered to the member at the desk beside him.

The room quieted and she continued. "—alleges certain breaches of privilege and contempts of the House by the Member for Fortune Bay-Cape La Hune."

All heads turned to Sullivan. His eyes grew wide. His face bloomed red. He was confused, as if he'd just been shaken from a deep sleep. "What? Dis about me?"

"The Honorable the Member for Fortune Bay-Cape La Hune will stand and await recognition before speaking," admonished the Speaker. Sullivan stood just as the Speaker gave the Government House Leader permission to continue. He sat down.

"Thank you, Speaker. Point of Privilege was provided to you last week, Speaker, and copies of this report were delivered to you and each member of this Chamber at the same time."

The Speaker nodded his agreement and she continued. "The investigation uncovered instances of falsified expense claims for a capital area office, claims of expenses for a non-existent constituency office, the offer of money to members and others in exchange for votes, a campaign tax credit scheme, and diverting campaign donations to fund personal expenses, among others. The specifics and their evidence are presented in full detail in the report.

"At a minimum, these are violations of the House Code of Conduct principles 1, 3, and 8, and of House Standing Order 17. They bring disrepute upon the House and tarnish its dignity. Some aspects of these findings may also constitute federal or provincial crimes, and will be referred to the authorities for their own scrutiny."

More murmurs carried through the House. "Order, please!" the Speaker counseled again.

She resumed. "Speaker, this report raises questions of privilege. Standing Order 34 requires questions of privilege to be considered immediately. I believe the next step is for you to determine prima facie. Thank you, Speaker." She sat down.

"Thank you, the Honorable the Member for Conception Bay South. You are correct. The determination of—"

Sullivan jumped up. He pounded his fist on the desk, tumbling his latte to the floor. He screamed first at the Speaker and then at the Government House Leader. "You make dese ridiculous accusations about me without even tellin' me? Dat ain't no way to treat a man with respect!"

"Order! Order! The Honorable the Member for Fortune Bay-Cape La Hune will await recognition!"

"I will not! Dis is a disgrace on you and de House of de people of this province!"

"Sergeant-at-Arms, remove the Member for Fortune Bay-Cape La Hune!" the Speaker called out.

The sergeant-at-arms rose from his seat. He stood a burly six feet six inches tall as he moved toward the center of the Chamber.

"Okay, I'll sit down," Sullivan huffed. "But I won't be happy 'bout it!" He sat.

The Sergeant-at-Arms returned to his place by the door. The ruckus among the other members died and the Speaker redirected his comments to Sullivan.

"The Honorable the Member for Fortune Bay-Cape La Hune, you may now address the facts and findings of the report."

Sullivan stood again. "Facts? Dose ain't no facts, she just made up that stuff! Dis is about nothing except finding somebody in de Opposition to smear, de Government just wanting to shut me up because dey don't like me keeping them in line. Well, it ain't gonna work. The Superior Court is gonna hear from me about this!" He sat down.

The Speaker responded. "As chair of the Management Commission, I can say that the report does indeed bear on the facts. These are clear violations of the House of Assembly Accountability, Integrity, and Administration Act and the Members' Resources and Allowances Rules. As to the report itself, I ask whether the Member for Fortune Bay-Cape La Hune has read it."

Sullivan stood. His staff's note to *Read this* flashed in his brain and he hesitated, then shouted, "Dat ain't any your business!" He sat down again.

"Then I ask again, does the Member for Fortune Bay-Cape La Hune wish to speak to the facts and findings?"

Sullivan stood and scowled, but he couldn't think of anything to say. He sat down again.

"Hearing none, after a thorough review of the facts in this matter, I determine that there has been a prima facie breach of privilege. Is there a motion to refer to the Committee on Privileges and Elections, or to the House for immediate debate?"

The Government's house leader stood.

"The Honorable the Member for Conception Bay South."

"Thank you, Speaker. I move the matter be referred immediately to the House for debate." She sat down.

"Is there a second?"

A long silence passed before anyone responded. The New Democratic Party Leader stood.

"The Honorable the Member for Humber-Bay of Islands."

"Thank you, Speaker. I second." The member sat.

"The motion for immediate House debate has been moved and seconded. Is it the pleasure of the House that this matter be referred to the House for immediate debate?"

A chorus of ayes arose from the Chamber.

"Opposed?"

A few scattered nays were heard.

"The motion carries. The Honorable the Member for Fortune Bay-Cape La Hune, do you wish to make a statement before removing yourself from the Chamber?"

Sullivan stood. “I ain’t leavin’!” He sat down.

“Sergeant-at-Arms, remove the Member for Fortune Bay-Cape La Hune.”

“Okay, I’ll go,” Sullivan huffed. He dragged his feet to the door. The Sergeant-at-Arms opened it and escorted Sullivan out. He sat Sullivan down on a bench in the hallway and towered over him. “Sit there until you’re summoned!” he commanded. Sullivan folded his arms across his chest and glowered at the floor. The sergeant returned to his chair.

Inside the Chamber, the debate over a suitable remedy for the breach ensued. Some members argued that the breach was no worse than the 1923 cover-up of legislative fees and public money used to fund lifestyle and reelection campaign expenses for Sir Richard Anderson Squires during his premiership. Or the more recent nearly House-wide scandal in which members had double-billed their constituency allowances, or used them to make politically-motivated donations, renovate personal property, or pay for personal items. They argued that neither of those scandals saw members suffer retribution from the assembly itself, and in keeping with those precedents neither should Sullivan.

Others argued that the House would be subject to ridicule if it didn’t dispense at least a minimal response, and suggested a reprimand from the Speaker.

Some accused the Commission of letting the Government overblow the seriousness of the offenses as a way to embarrass the Opposition. Still others argued that the House now had laws and explicit rules for matters like these, that the Management Commission staff were available to provide advice and answer questions from any member so requesting, that it conducted initial and refresher training courses for members, and that the members need only pay attention to what they were told. Their view was that the only just response would be to suspend the member from the Assembly.

The debate continued for thirty minutes more, at which time the Speaker intervened. "I remind the Chamber that it has other important business today, too. Is there a motion?"

The Government House Leader stood.

"The Honorable the Member for Conception Bay South," the Speaker acknowledged.

"Thank you, Speaker. I move the Member for Fortune Bay-Cape La Hune be suspended from the House indefinitely. Thank you." She sat down.

Murmurs rose again and the Speaker admonished them to order. "Is there a second?" he asked.

An uncomfortable silence followed. Finally, the Opposition House Leader stood to speak.

"The Honorable the Member for Bonavista."

"Thank you, Speaker." He paused and scanned the members' faces, probing for signs of minds made up and minds still in doubt about how they'd respond if someone were to second a motion to discipline a member of their party. Then he spoke.

"Honorable Members, Mr. Speaker. Suspending a member from this Chamber is a remedy rarely, if ever, used. And that is as it should be, for it is the gravest remedy we can administer. It says not just that the member has done something wrong, but that the member is so unfit to serve this House that a lesser remedy is no remedy at all. I draw your attention to Code of Conduct Principle 11, that we as members must promote and support all ten prior principles of the Code by leadership and example. In our deliberations today, I believe we must consider not just the allegations we have heard, but also the member's character, motivations, and conduct within and without this Chamber."

He paused while his eyes scanned the membership again. "Certainly, the breaches of privilege before us today are concerning enough as they stand. I would take no pride in chastising a member of my own Party, nor any other Member for that matter." He paused again as frustration took his face. "But for three years the conduct of the member in question both within and without this Chamber has been so egregious that I gladly make an exception. I second the motion of the Member for Conception Bay South." He sat down.

Voices grew suddenly loud and members jumped up on both sides of the aisle. Some on the Government side applauded and shouted "Hear, hear!" Opposition members pointed fingers and called out "Traitor!" The Speaker rose from his chair. "Order!" he shouted. "Order, I say!"

Gradually, voices calmed and the members began to take their seats. The Speaker remained standing as he scowled at the Assembly. "I remind the members that respect and decorum are to be the hallmarks of this Chamber at all times!"

When all members were seated and quiet had returned to the Chamber, he took his chair and began again. "The Chamber must move this matter to a close. Is it the pleasure of the House that the Member for Fortune Bay-Cape La Hune be suspended indefinitely from this Chamber?"

He heard ayes.

"Opposed?"

He heard nays.

The voice vote was too close to call. The Speaker weighed his options. He could call it as best he could. If three or more members stood, there would be a challenge and he'd have to call for a division, a recorded vote. But he knew few members would want their vote recorded publicly on a disciplinary matter, which meant most members would be unlikely to stand if he called in favor of the ayes. But Sullivan was known to have a few allies who might stand out of allegiance, and even now he could see certain Opposition members leaning toward one another talking secretly, probably plotting their next move. He also knew a significant number of members despised Sullivan, and they might stand if he called in favor of the nays.

He made his decision and called the result, then waited. Complete silence followed. Then one member stood. More silence. The Speaker waited. His eyes scanned the Chamber. A second member stood. He scanned the Chamber again. He watched a third member begin to rise, hesitate, then sit back down. Still he waited.

After a full minute had passed, he spoke. "Sergeant-at-Arms, bring in the Member for Fortune Bay-Cape La Hune."

The sergeant stood, opened the door, and called Sullivan in. "The Speaker requests your presence." He held open the door while Sullivan passed into the Chamber. Sullivan bowed as he passed in front of the Speaker again, then went to his desk.

"Please stand," the Speaker said. Sullivan stood.

The Speaker quietly cleared his throat. "It is the decision of this Chamber that you be suspended from this House indefinitely. You will have three days to clear your office. Your accounts will be suspended immediately. Thank you for your service to this date. I'm sure the Premier will call for a byelection as soon as feasible." He looked toward the Premier, who was nodding his head.

Sullivan couldn't believe what he was hearing. *Suspended? Dismissed? Put out into the rain like a mangy cat?* He fumed. His face glowed red and his fists clenched.

He stood up. “Dis is unconstitutional!” he screamed. He pounded the desk. “You got no right, and I ain’t going nowhere! ”

“Order!” the Speaker demanded.

“Order, yourself!” Sullivan shouted back.

The Speaker rolled his eyes. “Sergeant-at-Arms . . .”

The sergeant stood and moved toward Sullivan. Sullivan threw himself onto his desk and held on with arms and legs. The sergeant came up behind him. Sullivan clung harder. The sergeant squeezed Sullivan’s upper arms from behind and pulled him away. He winced as he was uprooted and screamed, “Ow!” His desk microphone screeched and his blotter fell to the floor.

He squirmed and twisted as the sergeant worked him toward the exit. The sergeant put his back to the door, pushed the latch handle down with his elbow, butt-pushed it open, and dragged Sullivan with him. In the hallway he pushed Sullivan toward the elevator. He pushed DOWN with his elbow and waited, Sullivan still squirming in his hands. When the elevator door opened, he pushed Sullivan inside, punched the button for the first floor, and stood menacingly outside. Sullivan folded his arms in defiance and scowled back at him. The door closed and the elevator began its descent.

By the time the sergeant returned to the Chamber, the Speaker had postponed until further notice the third reading of Sullivan’s bill and called for a ten minute recess. Some members were engaged in heated debate about the outcome of the vote, some were standing and stretching, others were already moving toward the door.

The Government House Leader stood and gathered her papers from her desk, then looked up at the only person sitting in the visitor gallery. She gave him a thumbs-up and a smile. He returned her smile and waved back.

As she left the Chamber, the man in the gallery removed a cell phone from the inside pocket of his navy blue sport coat and dialed. He loosened the knot of his gray necktie as he waited. An answer came on the fourth ring.

"Good afternoon. Fish and Wildlife Department."

"Mitchell Gregg, please," said the man in the gallery.

"One moment, I'll transfer you to that connection."

A few seconds passed, then he heard, "Mitchell Gregg here. Who'm I speakin' to?"

"Mr. Gregg, this is Damon Duffy, President of the Island Federation of Hunters and Outfitters. Minister Sullivan has just been dismissed from his position in the Assembly. I wonder if you'd like to work with me and certain members of the House to expand your department's predator-management program."

27

It was noon when Zach Thomas climbed eighteen steps to the landing of the Arts and Sciences Building at Sir Wilfred Grenfell College and entered its double glass door. His hair was trimmed and combed, his janitor's uniform was clean and freshly ironed, and his work shoes shined. His left hand carried a small box and his face beamed. He walked under the flags of indigenous and nation states, climbed the stairway, and continued down the long hallway lined with photographs of important-looking people on its walls. Something about one of them caught his attention and he stopped for a closer look.

The photograph showed a broadly smiling man of about his age with brown wavy hair, bushy eyebrows, and a full brown beard. He'd studied it intently before he realized why it had caught his attention. The man in the photograph looked a little bit like him—or, rather, how he thought he might have looked if life hadn't taken so much away. He reminded himself life was kinder now, but he sighed deeply anyway. *Would life have been different if I'd been born a day earlier? Or later? Or somewhere else? Or to someone else?* He wondered who could ever answer questions like that, then sighed again because the answers didn't matter anyway. He turned and continued down the hallway.

The smile returned to his face when he arrived at the room with this sign on the wall beside its door:

DEPARTMENT OF ENVIRONMENTAL STUDIES
OFFICE OF THE CHAIR
ANNAMARIE CHARTIER, PHD

The door was closed. He knocked politely and waited but he hoped no one was inside. *Must be at lunch*, he said to himself, then knocked again to be sure. When no answer came the second time, he quietly tried the knob. It was unlocked and he let himself in.

The room was as he remembered it. Flowers on the corner of her assistant's desk, artwork on the walls, comfortable chairs along the wall and behind the desk, bookcases with titles he didn't understand. He stopped for a moment to remember which of the chairs he'd sat in the first time he was here.

He walked past the desk and through an interior door to the office behind it. His eyes widened when he entered. He saw a large desk of dark wood with a padded armchair in front of it. On both sides of the desk's computer screen he saw framed pictures of people smiling. He guessed some of those pictures were of her with friends or family. For a second, images of his own brother and sister flashed before him. He remembered being only six when the three of them were taken away. He wondered where they were and if he'd ever see them again.

A bookcase and a file cabinet made of wood matching the desk stood against the wall across from the door. The window beside the desk looked out on a large grassy park with a sidewalk through the middle. In the center of the room stood an oval wooden table with padded leather chairs around it. Photographs of mountain scenery, small towns, and coastlines decorated the walls.

For a few moments he just stood there taking it all in. But he reminded himself why he had come and he resumed his work.

In the center of the round table sat a small, white, glass bowl filled with wrapped candies. He moved the bowl aside and set the box in its place. From the breast pocket of his uniform he removed a plain white card, leaned it against the side of the box, then stepped back. He smiled with satisfaction and hoped she would like it. As he turned to leave, he nearly ran into the woman standing behind him.

"By what means are you here, monsieur?" she demanded. "I have not requested a special cleaning!"

She was just his height, but the furrowed brow, the glare in her eyes, and the hands planted firmly on her hips made her seem much taller.

He lowered his head and looked down at the floor. *She doesn't remember.* "I'm sorry, ma'am. I just . . ." he stammered in a gravelly voice. His hand started to point to the box on the table.

"Just what, monsieur?" she interrupted. "These are private things in my office and must not be disturbed! I believe you should leave now! Must I call the security?"

"But . . ." he stammered again. He collected himself enough to reach for the card. He offered it to her.

She read her own name, hand-written. Her face softened. She bent slightly and studied his face. "Do ... do I know you, monsieur?"

He lifted his head. "Yes, ma'am. The box and the backpack I brought you from the lady in the accident? He pointed to the name stitched above his breast pocket. "Zach Thomas . . . remember?"

Her hand shot up over her mouth. “Oh my! Monsieur Thomas, really?” She studied his face again. “Oui, it is you! But I would not have recognized you! You look so—”

“Different? Yes, ma’am.”

Her eyes moved down his uniform to his shoes, then back up to his face and hair. “No, more than that, monsieur. You look well, very well indeed. And, I think, quite handsome, too,” she added matter-of-factly.

He smiled and blushed. “Thank you, ma’am. My life . . . you changed it.”

She returned a schoolteacher smile. “Ah, but that is where you are incorrect, monsieur. I simply gave an opportunity. You are the one who used it to advantage, that is all very plain to me. And you look to me very proud of yourself.”

“Yes, ma’am, I guess you could say I am.”

She turned her attention to the card in her hand. “And what is this?”

He slid the box to the edge of the table and offered it to her. “For you,” he said proudly.

She carried the box and the card with her, swiveled her desk chair around to face him, and sat down. “May I open this now?”

“Of course, ma’am.”

She opened the top flaps and peered inside. She removed a wooden figure with a paper tag tied to it. The tag read simply “Thank you from Zach Thomas” printed in pencil. She smiled up at him.

He clasped his hands behind his back and lowered his eyes. “I don’t know fancy words, ma’am. I’m just grateful about what you did for me.”

“This is very sweet, Zach Thomas. And it was my pleasure to have helped in any way.”

She studied the figure in her hand. It was about fifteen centimeters tall. Its body was carved in feathers, and its round head was slightly indented on the sides for its eyes. Its short, narrow bill was shaped like a broad arrowhead and stretched from throat to forehead. It stood tall and erect on webbed feet with chest puffed out. Its eyes focused squarely to the right, as if a sudden danger had caught its attention.

"Puffin," he said. "I carved it myself."

"Oui, our provincial bird! It is indeed most beautiful!" She placed it to the right of her monitor on top of a short stack of references and eyed it approvingly. "There, that is a good place." She smiled. "It will greet me every day."

"Yes, ma'am." But then his eyes drifted downward again. He was quiet for a long moment. "The lady in the accident," he said looking up again. "Is she okay?"

Dr. Chartier answered thoughtfully. "Oui, monsieur. I can say that a colleague of mine has visited her and that she is recovering very well."

His smile returned. "That's good. She seemed nice."

"Well . . ." He looked down again and shuffled his feet. ". . . I have to go. Classrooms to clean."

She stood and smiled. "It was very much my pleasure to see you again. The university does very well to have you in its employ. You will drop by again sometime, yes?"

"Yes, ma'am, when I can."

"Very good then, Zach Thomas." She offered him her hand and another smile. He shook her hand, thanked her again, then took a step forward and awkwardly pulled her toward him. She thought she saw a tear in his eye as he hugged her.

"Au revoir, Zach Thomas," she said, hugging him back.

"Bye, ma'am." He released her as quickly as he'd pulled her in, then turned and left.

As he disappeared down the hallway, she thought about how far he'd come with only the littlest bit of help, and how easy it was to do some good in this world if one only tried. That caused her to think about how many of her students had found their way with just the slightest bit of thoughtful advice. And that caused her to think about how much she'd miss the university, her colleagues and friends, the students she'd guided into their careers or advanced degrees, and the chance to do it again year after year. "Endlessly gratifying," was how she'd described that part of her job to anyone who'd been thoughtful enough to ask.

She moved to the window and stood before it with arms folded. Her eyes settled on the grassy park below, but her mind went elsewhere. It was called Bay d'Espoir Academy, just across the water from the Mi'kmaq Reserve. She'd be teaching college level sciences to the brightest in the high school's senior grade. It would last only a school year, but she wanted something new, an extended break from the stress of running a department—a holiday from having to do more with less every year. And it would give her and Peter time together, a chance to see where things might go for them. She couldn't wait to tell him.

28

May of the following year

Billy McCabe entered the front of a plain, single-story building of red brick and gray concrete on tree-lined Cromer Avenue. The sign in front said it was Grand Falls-Windsor's Provincial Court Centre, and its glass entrance doors reflected him dressed in an orange jumpsuit flanked by two men wearing the red serge of the RCMP.

The constables escorted him through the door and down the hallway to an oak bench. Billy sat as ordered, with a constable on each side of him. Not that Billy would have tried to run away; he would always have done what he was told to do.

It was very quiet. He stared at the large wooden door across the hallway. His hands fidgeted nervously in his lap because he remembered being on the other side of that door twice before.

The first time had been when a thin, white-haired judge had sat at a big desk at the front of the room. He'd worn a red and black robe and a white bow tie with long tails. He'd peered over the glasses on his nose and asked Billy, "How do you plead?"

Billy hadn't been sure what that meant, but his lawyer had reminded him to say "not guilty." Then his lawyer had asked the judge for what sounded to Billy like a sky-ski-atric exam. Billy had learned later that it meant a special doctor would give him tests and ask him a lot of questions.

The second time had been when he'd sat in the seat at the very front of that room while his lawyer and a lawyer he didn't know asked him questions about what he and Mr. S had done. The judge had sat at his big desk and listened. Billy remembered that the judge had sometimes asked questions, too, and that sometimes the lawyers had argued. He also remembered that the people sitting in the two rows at the side of the room had stared at him a lot. And when it was over, he'd been taken to a place called a halfway house.

Sitting on the oak bench now, he remembered how scared and nervous he'd been on both of those days. He felt scared and nervous now, too. He didn't want to answer so many questions again, or go back to that house either.

The glass doors of the front entrance opened again and Billy turned his head. Two men walked in. Billy recognized both of them as the lawyers who'd asked him questions the last time he had been in the room across the hallway. The one in the dark gray suit was Billy's lawyer. As he approached, one of the constables slid over to allow him to sit beside Billy. The other lawyer went to a different bench.

Billy's lawyer leaned in toward him. "We'll go inside in a minute or so," he said. "They're finishing up with another case now, and we'll be next. We'll sit in the back row until it's our turn to move up front. When it is, the judge will ask you to stand and say your name. Then you stay standing while the judge reads your sentence. Understand?"

Billy nodded even though he didn't.

"And don't worry, everything will be okay," the lawyer added. Billy looked down at his hands fidgeting in his lap and wondered how anything could be okay right now.

The large wooden door across the hallway opened and Billy startled. A woman leaned out and motioned for them to come in. They stood and followed her inside, and the other lawyer came behind them. Billy and his lawyer sat in the back row on the left side, while the other lawyer went to the right side.

To Billy's left sat a tall man with thinning hair dressed in a dark plaid shirt and denim overalls. A gray-striped ball cap hung on his knee. Billy remembered seeing him in this row before. The man smiled and nodded when Billy looked over at him. Billy nodded back but the smile he returned was only halfhearted.

Billy was shaking inside. He didn't understand why he had to be here again. All he wanted was to be out in the forest on his ATV doing his job. But he sat there and waited his turn anyway, just as he'd been told to do.

There was another man in an orange jumpsuit sitting at a small desk in front of the very front row. The judge asked him to stand and say his name. The man stood and answered but Billy couldn't understand what he said because the man was facing away from him.

Then the judge spoke. "You have been charged and convicted by jury of two counts of manslaughter, one count of assault with a weapon, and one count of aggravated assault. Do you have anything to say before I deliver your sentence?"

"Yeah, as a matter of fact I do, Judge." The man was talking a lot louder now.

"Please address this court as Your Honor," the judge admonished.

The man slammed his handcuffed fists onto the table in front of him. "No, I will not!" he yelled. "You're a fraud and this trial has been a sham from the start! You and your jury and your prosecutors are as complicit as everyone else! Your eyes are so closed that you do not see what so plainly happens before them! Your deafening silence enables the profiteers to take what they want from the Earth and leave behind their poisons and sludges and wastewaters! Steal the habitat from the land to make room for your condos and high rises! Harvest the fishes until they can no longer reproduce fast enough to sustain themselves!" He raised his voice another octave. "And allow precious wildlife to be killed off wherever they pose the smallest inconvenience!" He slammed his fists onto the table again. "Where is your heart, man? Where is your conscience?"

"Your remarks are noted," the judge said calmly. He coughed quietly into his fist then lowered his eyes to read from a prepared document. "It is the judgement of this court that you shall serve nine years for each of two counts of manslaughter on the lives of Leon John and Rod Penny, eight years for assault with a weapon on the life of Carson Sullivan, and ten years for aggravated assault on the life of Peter Joe, for a total of thirty-six years. Eligibility for parole begins not before you have fully served one-third of your sentence.

"This court notes that you have also been charged with federal crimes and numerous violations of provincial administrative code. Those charges will be dealt with in other courts. You're dismissed. Bailiff, remove the prisoner from this courtroom." The judge tapped his gavel onto its oaken pad.

The bailiff took the prisoner by the right arm and tried to turn him toward the aisle. He jerked his arm free, turned back to the judge, and scowled. "This isn't over! I won't be defeated!" he yelled.

The judge hammered his gavel onto its pad and raised his voice. "Bailiff, remove the prisoner!" The bailiff grabbed the prisoner's upper arms from behind and muscled him into the aisle and toward the door.

Billy's eyes widened and he gasped as they reached his row. "Mr. S!" he cried out.

Ross Nelson fought his captor to face Billy. He scowled and spat on the floor. The bailiff tightened his grip and once again pushed him forward. He bent his head back over his shoulder and shouted at Billy, "Some help you were, idiot!"

Billy had always tried to do his best at his job. He didn't know why Mr. S would be mad at him now, but it sounded like Mr. S had scolded him again. Billy had been called that word before and he didn't like it. He thought about how much he didn't want to work for Mr. S anymore. But when he tried to think about where else he could work he couldn't think of any other place. He sighed out loud and looked down at his hands fidgeting in his lap again.

As the bailiff pushed Nelson those final steps toward the door, the courtroom became quiet again. Nelson was too busy struggling to notice Mitchell Gregg sitting next to reporter Emma Walsh with a notebook in her lap snapping photos of him from the last row.

Billy heard the judge clear his throat again and he looked up. "Next case!" he heard.

"That's us," Billy's lawyer said as he stood up. Billy followed him to the small desk in front of the front row where they both sat down. A new bailiff took the place of the first one.

The judge shuffled some papers on his desk, asked Billy to stand, and addressed him directly. "State your name for the record, please."

"Billy McCabe," he answered.

"Mr. McCabe, you have been charged with two counts of manslaughter. Do you have anything to say before we continue?"

Billy looked at his lawyer then shook his head. "No, sir."

"Please address this court by Your Honor."

"Yes, sir. Your Honor, sir."

"Thank you, young man." He turned to the bailiff. "Call in the jury, please."

The bailiff disappeared through a door at the side of the courtroom. Moments later, he returned and held the door open. One by one, twelve people entered the jurors' box and seated themselves.

The judge turned to the juror seated closest to him. "Madame Foreperson, may we have the verdict, please."

The foreperson stood and read from the sheet of paper in her hand. "Your Honor, the jury finds the defendant, Mr. Billy McCabe, not criminally responsible as charged by reason of a mental disorder of sufficient magnitude as to adversely influence his judgement and behavior."

"Thank you, Madam Foreperson." She seated herself again.

The judge shuffled more papers. He removed his glasses and set them aside. He leaned into folded hands and elbows on his desk, and looked Billy directly in the eye. "Mr. McCabe, do you understand the jury's verdict?"

Billy looked at his lawyer. The lawyer nodded at Billy. Billy looked back at the judge. "Yes, sir . . . I mean Your Honor."

"Very good, then. Mr. McCabe, given your verdict it is my judgement that it is in the province's best interest to withdraw the charges filed against you and that your record be expunged, with one condition. I have discussed your case with the provincial Mental Health Court, and it is our mutual judgement that you would benefit from its services."

The judge looked past Billy and his lawyer at the benches behind them. "Is Mr. Graham Brodie in the courtroom?"

Billy and his lawyer turned around. The man in the dark plaid shirt and denim overalls was now standing with his cap in his hand.

"Please come forward, Mr. Brodie."

The man sidestepped into the aisle, and strode to the front beside Billy.

"Mr. McCabe, this is Mr. Brodie. Mr. Brodie, this is Mr. McCabe."

Graham Brodie reached out to shake Billy's hand and smiled at him. "It's a pleasure, young man."

"Very good," the judge resumed. "Mr. McCabe, Mr. Brodie here is a long-time counselor known well to this court. He operates the Rattling Brook Therapy Farm. Mr. Brodie, tell Mr. McCabe about it."

Graham Brodie turned to Billy. "We're an operating farm. Fifteen people including me and my wife, but we're all family there. We raise cattle and sheep on one hundred fifty hectares in the upper reaches of Great Rattling Brook, and organic fruit and vegetables in our greenhouses. We need people to help with that, and with fencing, landscaping, and maintaining equipment. You'll get paid, of course. My wife and I live in the house, but you'll have your own bunkhouse like all the others do.

"We can arrange training for you in the skilled trades, like welding, carpentry, and construction. You'd get paid for that, too. Get certified, or just be an all-round handy man if you want to. It's good training either way.

"I've been following your case, young man." He put his hand on Billy's shoulder. "What I've read and seen of you tells me you've got a good work ethic and a strong desire to learn. And you're honest, kind, and respectful—good qualities I don't always find in people. We'd love to have you join us."

The judge took over again. "So, what do you think, Mr. McCabe?"

Billy looked at Graham Brodie. "Can I send some money to my mom?"

Graham Brodie smiled. "I think we can arrange that, son."

Billy looked to his lawyer, who gave him a smile and a thumbs up, then at Graham Brodie again and then at the judge. His face relaxed. "I think I'd like that, Your Honor."

"Very good then. I've placed only one condition on your case, and that is that you apply to the Mental Health Court for assistance and avail yourself of its services for a period not less than one year, after which your charges will be withdrawn and your record cleared. You'll need to file a formal application with that court to start. My strong recommendation will be that you be placed at Mr. Brodie's farm. No guarantee you'll get it, but they've heeded my suggestions in the past. And I'm sure Mr. Brodie will have a word with them, too. And last thing, you must report to that court within twenty days. You're free to go home until then. No need to stay in that halfway house any longer.

"So, if there are no more questions—" He paused while his eyes scanned from Billy, to Graham Brodie, to Billy's lawyer. "—this case is concluded and you are dismissed, Mr. McCabe." He tapped the gavel onto its pad.

Billy, his lawyer, and Graham Brodie thanked the judge, turned into the aisle, and headed for the door. Billy relaxed and took a deep breath. The shaking inside had stopped and he smiled as he walked. He smiled so much that he didn't notice Emma Walsh in the last row photographing him, too.

They were nearly to the door when the judge called out, "Oh, Mr. McCabe!" All three of them turned around. Billy's eyes widened and his brow rose, wondering what kind of trouble he was in now.

"I forgot one thing. Get your lawyer to find you some decent clothes." He winked at Billy. "That orange thing doesn't suit you."

As the three of them left the courtroom, Emma gathered her camera and notebook, and she and Mitchell followed them at a comfortable distance. Outside, they stood by the door and watched them drive away. A feeling of contentment grew within Emma and she smiled. "Life has its ways, Mitchell."

29

I returned to my office and sighed at the piles on my desk. The latest challenge to our hunting and fishing rights had failed, but only after nearly eight months of repeated onslaughts in the form of motions and counter-motions, dismissals and judgements, weariness within our negotiating team, and frustration among all of our people. It had also left me with an enormous filing job.

I still wondered how this challenge could have been filed so many years after we had all come to believe our rights had been settled. It had begun shortly after the deaths of Leon, the Kitpu, and Rod Penny, and I now realized I had pushed the pain, anger, and confusion of those days deep inside in order to focus where I was needed. It was time to sit with the Old Ones, time to find answers, time to heal. I decided to go where I hadn't gone for far too long.

I climbed the path to the Sacred Ground. I sat on a boulder and looked out over the still water of Bay d'Espoir stretching out before me. It was evening, but the bay still reflected the sun low on the horizon. I felt the privilege of being awed by our Mother Earth; her presence touched me from every direction. I closed my eyes and heard the trees, the water, the rocks, and the animals speak. I imagined myself in the time of Kluscap as he prepared the Earth for my people, created us from arrows shot into ash trees, and taught us how to live.

I opened my eyes and turned around. Fall had dried the grasses and colored the leaves a red-brown. I stood and walked among the pyramids, aware that the Old Ones were everywhere around me. Joes, Jeddores, Sylliboys, and many others. Those who had led my people from Unama'kik to make a new Mi'kmaq nation here on Ktaqamkuk, and those that had guided us so thoughtfully ever since.

I walked to the center of the pyramids, then continued slightly beyond. The pyramid standing before me looked the same as all the others, but this one was etched deep in my memory. I had arrived at my father's grave.

I stood there for a few moments, trying to not think, to not feel anything. I closed my eyes again and listened to the sounds around me—the rustle of leaves, the buzz of a fly, the wingbeat of a raven, the chuck of a red squirrel.

But try as I did, my mind could not let go of its questions, nor my heart of its pain. *What had really happened in those weeks? What was achieved? A beloved grandfather and Elder and another man dead, the grief of family members, four eagles poisoned, one man imprisoned, a disabled man drawn into a crime, and who knows how many coyotes and wolves taken by those devices . . . for what? To exert man's will over nature? For advantage over others? For celebrity or prestige? When will people learn that none of these matter? That what matters is the common good of all on Mother Earth, of which humans are only a part no more or less important than any other!*

I waited for answers, but none came. I entreated the Old Ones again. I called to my father. Still no answer. I grew frustrated and I huffed out my anger at the selfishness of the human race. Minutes passed before I accepted that I would be hearing no answer today. I opened my eyes and turned to leave.

That was when I saw them—a gray-brown female coyote and two nearly grown, pure white pups only meters away. I had heard about snow coyotes. It was a gene anomaly more common here on Ktaqamkuk than anywhere else. No one seemed to know why.

The female sat perfectly still, just watching me. The pups sniffed the grass around them, then sat beside her and watched me, too. I did not know how long they had been there, but they stayed even as I watched them, as if they knew I posed no threat. Then the adult stood, turned away, and gave a quiet, high-pitched bark. The pups followed and in only seconds they disappeared into the grasses.

That's when I realized I'd been given my answer. "We're still here," they'd said to me.

END

Glossary

Mi'kmaw terms

E'e -- Yes[2]

Gwitji'j – Son.[8]

Jipuji'j – Jipuji'jkuei Kuespem Provincial Park

Kitpu – The eagle, a sacred bird. Kitpu carries Mi'kmaw prayers to Kji-Niskam. (Also Gitpu.)[7,8]

Kji-Niskam – The Great Spirit; the creator of everything. (Also Gisoolg, Kji'Kinap.)[10]

Kji-Saqamaw – A hereditary Grand Chief.[10]

Kluscap – Kluscap created the animals and birds from dirt and stone. Kluscap created the human beings from four arrows shot into ash trees, and taught them how to live in the world. (Also Glooscap, Gluscap, Elder Brother.)[3]

Ktaqamkuk – The island of Newfoundland. (Also Ugtaqamgug.)[1]

Kwe' – Hello or Greetings[2]

Mi'kma'ki – The land of the Mi'kmaq.[2]

Mi'kmaq – The Indigenous people of Canada's maritime provinces.[7]

Mi'kmaw – The singular form of Mi'kmaq.[9]

Mi'kmawisimk – The language of the Mi'kmaq.[7]

Moque -- No[2]

Niskamij – Grandfather.[2]

Pa'si – Sit down[2]

Pjila'si – Welcome[8]

Piskwa' – Come in[2]

Salite – A celebration or feast in honor of one who has recently passed away, often followed by an auction to help the grieving family with burial costs.[11]

Saqamaw – A hereditary Chief.[8]

Spirit's Road – The silver path of stars to the Next World; the Milky Way.[6]

Unama'kik – Cape Breton, Nova Scotia.[2]

Wela'lin – Thank you (directed to one person).[2]

Wela'lioq – Thank you (directed to more than one person).[2]

Weliaq – You're welcome (Also It is good, or That's good).[2]

Weli eksitpu'k – Good morning[2]

Newfoundland terms

Barasway – A shallow estuary, lagoon, or harbour on the island of Newfoundland sheltered from the sea by a sand bar or narrow strip of land.[4]

Barrens – An elevated land or plateau with low, scrubby vegetation.[4]

B'y – A slang form of "boy," pronounced like a short "bye." Now, an informal term of address for a male of any age. In the former British fishery of Newfoundland, a b'y was an inexperienced man on his first voyage.[4]

Come from away – A phrase referring to someone who visits or moves to Canada's maritime provinces from somewhere else.[14]

Outport – Any coastal community in Newfoundland and Labrador other than St. John's.[4]

Pond – A lake.[4]

Screech – A Jamaican rum bottled in Newfoundland and Labrador.[4]

The Rock – An affectionate name for the island of Newfoundland.[5]

Tuckamore – Small, stunted evergreens with gnarled spreading roots forming closely matted ground-cover on the barrens; low stunted vegetation; scrub.[4]

General terms

Kilometer – Approximately six-tenths of a mile. One hundred kilometers is approximately sixty-two miles.

Meter – Three and one-third feet. Ten meters is approximately eleven yards.

Riding – An electoral district in Canada.[13]

Glossary Sources

1. People of the Dawn Indigenous Friendship Centre, "A Glimpse into Ktaqamkuk Mi'kmaw History: Indigenous Peoples of Newfoundland." (St. John's, Newfoundland and Labrador: Municipalities NL, n.d.) https://municipalnl.ca/site/uploads/2021/11/New-Ktaqmkuk-Mikmaq-History-PPT.pdf

2. Aboriginal Language Initiative, www.firstnationhelp.com/ali/.

3. Stephen Augustine, narrator, "Mi'kmaq Creation Story," told at Elsipogtog (Big Cove), New Brunswick (Gaitineau, QC: Canadian Museum of History, n.d.)

https://www.historymuseum.ca/wp-content/uploads/2020/06/Mikmaq-Creation-Story-EN.pdf

4. *Dictionary of Newfoundland English* (Toronto: University of Toronto Press, 1982, 1983)

5. Encounter Newfoundland Online, "Newfinese: 101 Words and Phrases You're Likely to Hear on the Rock," 2023, https://encounternewfoundland.com/newfinese-101-words-and-phrases-youre-liketo-hear-on-the-rock/

6. Bernard Gilbert Hoffman, "Excerpts from the Hoffman Thesis – Mi'kmaq of the 16th & 17th Centuries," *The Historical Ethnography of the Micmac of the Sixteenth and Seventeenth Centuries, 1955*. From Cape Breton University, 2023, accessed online at https://www.cbu.ca/indigenous-affairs/mikmaq-resource-centre/mikmaq-resource-guide/essays/excerpts-from-the-hoffman-thesis-mikmaq-of-the-16th-17th-centuries/

7. Benoit First Nation, "L'nui'sin" (De Grau, NL: Benoit First Nation, n.d.) accessed online at benoitfirstnation.ca/bfn_language.html

8. Mi'gmaq Mi'kmaq Online Talking Dictionary, n.d., accessed online at https://www.mikmaqonline.org

9. Nova Scotia Museum, "Spelling of Mi'kmaq" (Nova Scotia Museum: Mi'kmaq Portraits Collection, n.d.) accessed online at https://novascotia.ca/museum/mikmaq/?section=spelling#:~:text=The%20term%20Mi'kmaq%2C%20is,never%20used%20as%20an%20adjective

10. Muin'iskw (Jean) and Crowfeather (Dan), "Mikmaw Spirit," website (updated April 2020), accessed online at https://www.muiniskw.org/index.htm

11. Luisa Martin, "Salite: A Mi'kmaq Sacred Tradition," online slideshow (Prezi website, March 20, 2014) https://prezi.com/ocrrwhqk7vuu/salite-a-mikmaq-sacred-tradition/

12. The Canadian Encyclopedia, website, funded by the Government of Canada, 2023, accessed online at https://www.thecanadianencyclopedia.ca

13. The Dictionary of Canadian Politics, website, (Campbell Strategies, Inc., 2023) accessed online at https://parli.ca/riding/

14. *The MacMillan Dictionary*, accessed online at https://www.macmillandictionary.com/us/dictionary/american/

About the Author

Photo by Tara Griesbach

It would be no exaggeration to say that I eagerly read every one of Tony Hillerman's mysteries set on the Navajo Nation while they were still warm. I can't explain what it was about them. I can only say that where I might be distracted only a few pages into any other novel, I would often finish a Tony Hillerman in a single evening, trying to solve it before Navajo police officers Joe Leaphorn, Jim Chee, or Bernadette Manuelito did. They were enthralling stories.

So it was that Tony Hillerman became the inspiration for writing my own mysteries. I hope you will enjoy trying to solve them before Peter Joe does.

— E. W.

E. W. Finke writes from knowledge acquired during almost thirty-five years of experience with the U.S. Environmental Protection Agency, including work with Native American nations. He later trained and worked briefly as a mediator and facilitator specializing in environmental matters. He has now turned that experience to writing environmental crime fiction.

Coyote's Wail is his second novel. *The Sweet Bounty* is his first. Both are set on the Canadian island of Newfoundland, a fascinating place he fell in love with during his first visit in 2001, and a place he has returned to many times since.

He makes his home in Bellingham, Washington, with his wife, Nadine, his dog, Buster, and his cat, Turmeric. He enjoys spending as much time outdoors as he possibly can.

Milton Keynes UK
Ingram Content Group UK Ltd.
UKHW040742290924
1898UKWH00016BA/24